THE TRANSLATORS

THE WOOD DEMON, the first collaboration of translators Nicholas Saunders and Frank Dwyer, will have its premiere at the Mark Taper Forum in Los Angeles in the spring of 1994. Mr. Dwyer, Literary Manager of the Taper, will direct members of the Antaeus Company in the production. Their second translation, Mikhail Bulgakov's ZOYA'S APARTMENT, commissioned by Circle in the Square and produced in the 1989-1990 Broadway season, has been published by Samuel French.

In a distinguished career as actor and director, Mr. Saunders has appeared in 19 Broadway shows and hundreds of televison programs, but is perhaps best remembered as Captain Barker in the old Phil Silvers "Sergeant Bilko" series. He played the role of Chubukov in the 1990 premiere of his own translation of Chekhov's THE MARRIAGE PROPOSAL. A native Russian, Mr. Saunders had a parallel career in the Russian language field, rising to be Production and Presentation Manager of the Russian Department at Radio Liberty. He proudly claims four generations of actors in his happy family.

Mr. Dwyer, formerly a member of such classical companies as the Repertory Theater of Lincoln Center and CSC Repertory Theater, is currently a member of the Antaeus Company at the Taper. Credits include Broadway, the New York Shakespeare Festival, Playwrights Horizons, Roundabout, and the Quaigh. Formerly Artistic Director of the Yankee Repertory Theater (off-off-Broadway) and a prizewinning poet, he has also written young adult biographies of DANTON, KING HENRY VIII, KING JAMES I, and JOHN ADAMS. He is married to actress-writer Mary Stark.

Smith and Kraus *Books For Actors*

THE MONOLOGUE SERIES
The Best Men's Stage Monologues of 1992
The Best Men's Stage Monologues of 1991
The Best Men's Stage Monologues of 1990
The Best Women's Stage Monologues of 1992
The Best Women's Stage Monologues of 1991
The Best Women's Stage Monologues of 1990
One Hundred Men's Stage Monologues from the 1980's
One Hundred Women's Stage Monologues from the 1980's
Street Talk: Character Monologues for Actors
Uptown: Character Monologues for Actors
Monologues from Contemporary Literature: Volume I
Monologues from Classic Plays
Kiss and Tell: The Art of the Restoration Monologue
FESTIVAL MONOLOGUE SERIES
The Great Monologues from the Humana Festival
The Great Monologues from the EST Marathon
The Great Monologues from the Women's Project
The Great Monologues from the Mark Taper Forum
YOUNG ACTORS SERIES
Great Scenes and Monologues for Children
New Plays from A.C.T.'s Young Conservatory
Great Scenes for Young Actors from the Stage
Great Monologues for Young Actors
SCENE STUDY SERIES
The Best Stage Scenes for Women from the 1980's
The Best Stage Scenes for Men from the 1980's
The Best Stage Scenes of 1992
PLAYS FOR ACTORS SERIES
Seventeen Short Plays by Romulus Linney
Lanford Wilson: 21 Short Plays
William Mastrosimone: Collected Plays
Eric Overmeyer: Collected Plays
Terrence McNally: Collected Plays
OTHER BOOKS IN OUR COLLECTION
The Actor's Chekhov
Women Playwrights: The Best Plays of 1992
Humana Festival '93: The Collected Plays
Break A Leg! Daily Inspiration for the Actor

If you require pre-publication information about upcoming Smith and Kraus
monologues collections, scene collections, play anthologies, advanced acting
books, and books for young actors, you may receive our semi-annual
catalogue, free of charge, by sending your name and address to **Smith and
Kraus Catalogue, P.O. Box 10, Newbury, VT 05051.**

❖

THE WOOD DEMON

(Lyeshiy)

A Comedy
in Four Acts by
Anton Pavlovich Chekhov

translated by
Nicholas Saunders and Frank Dwyer

Great Translations for Actors Series

A Smith and Kraus Book

❖

A Smith and Kraus Book
Published by Smith and Kraus, Inc.
802-866-5423

COVER AND TEXT DESIGN BY JULIA HILL
Manufactured in the United States of America

First Edition: March 1993
10 9 8 7 6 5 4 3 2 1

Library of Congress Cataloging-in-Publication Data
Chekhov, Anton Pavlovich, 1860 - 1904.
    [Leshii. English]
    The wood demon / by Anton Chekhov ; [translated by Nicholas Saunders
    and Frank Dwyer]. -- 1st ed.
       p. cm.
    "Great translations for actors."
    ISBN 1-880399-30-X
    I. Saunders, Nicholas. II. Dwyer, Frank. III. Title.
    PG3456.L5S28 1993   93-21865
    891.72 ' 3--dc20   CIP

Contents

❖

❖

PUBLISHER'S PREFACE

Those who wish to read the great works of a foreign literature must learn the language or depend on the kindness of translators; and every translation must try to recover both the letter and the spirit of the original. Translators must know two languages so intimately that it's more than a metaphor to call it "by heart." They must also have some writer's instinct to understand how best to recreate the essence of the original work, from the most seemingly spontaneous elements of its style to the most profound of its ideas.

The sense of a work is more easily translated than its particular sound, and we may apprehend the narrative or the ideas of the original even as we complain that it all sounds "like a translation." The hardest task of the translator is to determine what in the very language of a piece makes it sound like Chaucer, or Dickens, or Joyce, and then discover how those qualities can be recapitulated in a different language. It don't mean a thing, alas, if it ain't got that swing.

There are singular problems in attempting to translate works for the theater. Special care must be taken to make the work sound right—and Molière does not sound like Racine. Care must also be taken, however, to make the lines easy for actors to speak: a play is a live experience in which a reality is conjured that must include the unforced participation of actors and audiences. Care must also be taken to preserve the particular flavor of the individual characters: old men, for example, don't have the same vocabularies and rhythms as young girls. In addition, the language of the translation should give us something of the time and the place of the original play.

Smith and Kraus aspires to bring great plays from other countries and cultures into new, vital, and eminently actable American translations. For too long, high school and college productions of Ibsen or Chekhov, for example, have put a distorting screen of British sensibility between the great playwrights, on the one side, and our actors and audiences on the other, because of British translations. It is absurd, but unhappily not uncommon, for young American actors playing servants and lower class types to struggle with Cockney accents in Norwegian or Russian plays.

This new translation of Anton Chekhov's little known masterpiece, THE WOOD DEMON, has been made by two men of the theater, Nicholas Saunders and Frank Dwyer. Mr. Saunders is a native Russian whose command of both Russian and English gave him parallel careers as a Broadway and television performer and as a Russian-language producer at Radio Liberty. Mr. Dwyer, a poet, is also an accomplished actor and director. There is no hint here of oldfashioned translationese, with all the characters sounding awkwardly alike. Instead, as you will see, THE WOOD DEMON leaps with a kind of life it has not had before, in English.

"Translations for actors": we here at Smith & Kraus take our motto very seriously. We promise you that the translations we bring you will be so faithful, fresh, and eloquent you will want to read the plays out loud. Crafted especially for production, they will help you plunge deep inside the original work. They will never block your way.

ACKNOWLEDGMENTS

The Antaeus Company was founded in December, 1990, by Dakin Matthews and Lillian Garrett-Groag, under the aegis of Gordon Davidson, Artistic Director/Producer of the Mark Taper Forum, to explore the possibility of creating a permanent classical repertory ensemble in Los Angeles. The Taper gave the Antaeus Company a Classics Lab workshop of THE WOOD DEMON at its developmental space in the John Anson Ford Theater in the spring of 1992: a two-and-a half week rehearsal period culminating in three open public rehearsals. The translators and the Antaeus Company wish to express their deepest thanks to Gordon Davidson.

The translators also wish to thank Mary Scoville, Penny Fuller, Lillian Garrett-Groag, Oskar Eustis, Christopher Breyer, and Renee Leask.

This translation will have its premiere at the Mark Taper Forum, with the Antaeus Company under the direction of Frank Dwyer, in the spring of 1993-94 season.

Act I

and two or three guests.)

Come! Please! Begin! Help yourselves! *(He gestures to the small table.)* The Serebryakovs haven't arrived. There's no Fyodor Ivanich, no Wood Demon. Everyone has forgotten us.

YULYA: Will you have some vodka, Godfather dear?

ORLOVSKY: Just a drop. That's it...enough!

DYADIN: *(Tying a napkin around his neck.)* Everything is so perfect here, Yuliya Stepanovna! When I come past your fields, or stroll through your shady garden, or look at this table – everywhere I can see the supreme authority of your magical little hand. To your health!

YULYA: But there are so many things to worry about, Ilya Ilyich. Yesterday, for example, Nazarka failed to round up our turkeys and get them back into the barn. They slept out here, in the garden, in the cold night air. And now today, five of the little ones are gone.

DYADIN: Oh, that should never be! The turkey is a delicate bird.

VOYNITSKY: *(To Dyadin.)* Slice me some ham, Waffles.

DYADIN: With great pleasure. What a beautiful ham! Right out of "The Arabian Nights." *(Carving.)* For you, Zhorzhinka, I'll carve by all the rules of the art – neither Beethoven nor Shakespeare could carve any better – but not with this knife. *(He sharpens the knives together.)*

ZHELTOUKHIN: *(Wincing.)* Wa...Wa...Waffles! Stop it! I can't take it!

ORLOVSKY: Well, Yegor Petrovich, tell us, what's going on at your house?

VOYNITSKY: Nothing is going on.

ORLOVSKY: What's new?

VOYNITSKY: Nothing. Everything is old. Everything is exactly the same as it was last year. I talk a lot, as usual, and do very little. My old jaybird of a mother, my *maman*, chatters on and on about the emancipation of women. She keeps one eye on the grave, and with the other searches through her wise little booklets for the dawn of a new life.

ORLOVSKY: And Sasha?

VOYNITSKY: Unfortunately, the professor has not yet been devoured by moths. As usual, from early morning till late at night, he sits in his study and writes: "Wracking our brains, knitting our brows, ode after ode we write;/ And no praise, either for us or for them, do we hear." Pity the paper he writes on! Sonichka, as usual, reads intellectual books and keeps a very intellectual diary.

ORLOVSKY: My dear little girl, my darling...

VOYNITSKY: With my keen powers of observation, I should be writing a novel. The story is begging to be told. A retired professor, dry as a crust, a learned beetle...gout, rheumatism, migraine, liver, all sorts of things...as jealous as Othello ...lives – reluctantly – on his first wife's country estate because he can't afford to live in the city...complains constantly about his misfortunes, although in reality he is the luckiest of men.

ORLOVSKY: Is that a fact?

VOYNITSKY: Of course. Just think, what luck! Let's not even mention that his father was a lowly deacon, that he himself only went to a second rate crown college run by the priests, where he nevertheless managed to get his degrees and his professor's chair, and now is "His Excellency," the son-in-law of a government minister, and so on: all that doesn't matter. What *does* matter is that for exactly 25 years a man has been reading and writing about art without understanding a thing about art! For 25 years he has been chewing on other people's ideas of realism, of "trends" and "tendencies" and other such stupidities. For 25 years he has been reading and writing about things that intelligent people already know and that stupid people aren't even interested in. In other words, for 25 years he's kept himself perpetually busy accomplishing absolutely nothing. And yet, what success! What renown! Why? For what? By what right?

Act I

ORLOVSKY: *(Roaring with laughter.)* Envy! Envy!

VOYNITSKY: Yes, envy!...And look at his success with women. No Don Juan ever enjoyed such total success. His first wife, my sister, a beautiful, gentle creature, pure as this blue sky, honorable, generous, who had more admirers than he had students, loved him as only angels can love other creatures as pure and beautiful as themselves. My mother, his mother-in-law, adores him to this day, and to this day he inspires in her a kind of holy awe. His second wife, bright, a beauty – you've seen her – married him when he was already old: she gave him her youth, her beauty, her freedom, her radiance. Why? For what? And what a talented pianist she is! She's an artist! How she can play!

ORLOVSKY: In fact, it's quite a talented family, a remarkable family.

ZHELTOUKHIN: Yes. Sofya Aleksandrovna, for instance, has a marvelous voice. An amazing soprano. I have never heard anything like it, not even in Petersburg. But, you know, she forces a little at the top. What a shame! Give me the high notes! Give me the high notes! If she only had them, then I swear to you, on my life, that she would be the most extraordinary singer. Do you know what I mean?...Excuse me, my friends, I have to talk to Yulya. *(He takes her aside.)* Send a messenger. Write that if they can't come now, at least they should come for dinner. *(More quietly.)* And don't be stupid. Don't embarrass me with your spelling. "Dinner" with two "n's." *(Louder, with tenderness.)* I'll really appreciate this.

YULYA: Of course. *(She leaves.)*

DYADIN: They say that the professor's wife, Yelena Andreyevna, whom I do not have the honor of knowing, is remarkable not only for her inner beauty, but for her outer beauty, as well.

ORLOVSKY: Yes, she is a glorious woman.

ZHELTOUKHIN: Is she faithful to her professor?

VOYNITSKY: Unfortunately, yes.

ZHELTOUKHIN: Why unfortunately?

VOYNITSKY: Because that fidelity is false from beginning to end. It sounds wonderful, but it doesn't make a bit of sense. To betray an old husband when your soul despises him is immoral. But to betray your own youth and your own true feelings is not immoral. Where the devil is the logic in that?

DYADIN: *(Tearfully.)* Zhorzhinka, I don't like you to talk this way. There, you see – I'm trembling! Gentlemen, I do not possess the gift of eloquence, but allow me without well-turned phrases to convey to you from my heart...Gentlemen, whoever is unfaithful to wife or husband is a traitor – and might just as well betray his homeland!

VOYNITSKY: Turn off the fountain!

DYADIN: Please, Zhorzhinka...Ivan Ivanich, Lyonichka, my dear friends, consider the vicissitudes of my unhappy lot. It's no secret and not veiled in mystery that my wife, on the day after our wedding, ran away with the man she loved, on the grounds of my unappealing appearance.

VOYNITSKY: And she was right!

(Laughter.)

DYADIN: Please, gentlemen! In spite of all that, I did not shirk my duty. I love her still! I am faithful to her, and I help her as much as I can. I have made my will and am leaving everything to the unsanctified little ones she had with her beloved. I have not shirked my duty, and I'm proud of it. Yes, proud! I have lost my happiness, but I have preserved my pride. And what about her? Her youth is gone; her beauty, in accordance with the laws of nature, has faded; the man she loved, may he rest in peace, is dead. And what does she have left. *(He sits.)* This is a serious matter, and you are laughing.

ORLOVSKY: You're a good man, you have a beautiful soul, but you talk too much, and you wave your arms about...

(Fyodor Ivanovich comes out of the house. He is wearing a fine poddiovka, a long overgarment narrow at the waist, with pleats; high boots; all sorts of medals and ribbons on his chest; a massive gold chain

Act I

profession is to yoke the wild elements and compel the stormy waves to turn the wheels of the mill, which I rent from my friend Wood Demon.

VOYNITSKY: Turn off the fountain, Waffles!

DYADIN: With great reverence, I bow before the luminaries of science *(He bows.)*, who adorn and extend the horizons of our Mother Russia. Forgive my impertinence, but I dream of visiting Your Excellency, and of delighting my soul with a chat about the latest scientific advances!

SEREBRYAKOV: Please. I will be happy to see you.

SONYA: Well, Godfather dear, tell us all about it! Where did you spend the winter? Where have you been hiding?

ORLOVSKY: Well, my dear, I was in Gmunden, Paris, Nice, London. I was in...

SONYA: Good for you, you lucky man!

ORLOVSKY: Come away with me in the autumn. Would you like that?

SONYA: *(Singing.)* "Don't tempt me unless you mean it..."

FYODOR IVANOVICH: Don't sing at the table, or your husband's wife will be a booby.

DYADIN: It would be so interesting to look at this table *a vol d'oiseaux*, to have a bird's-eye view! What a glorious bouquet! Grace, beauty, knowledge, tal...

FYODOR IVANOVICH: *(Interrupting.)* What magnificent language! Such eloquence...As if someone were running a carpenter's plane down your back. *(Laughter.)* "Hold your tongue and eat your pie."

SEREBRYAKOV: "Hold your tongue and eat your pie." Yes...in connection with this old saying, a little episode comes to mind. A certain professor – I don't think it's necessary for me to tell you his name – asked me to come and have lunch with him when I was in St. Petersburg. When the day came, I rode

The Wood Demon

over to his country villa, and whom did I find there but our late Sergey Mikhaylovich Solovyov. As we had both arrived early, our host made an effort to entertain us by discoursing on the subject of social outcasts in early Russian history. Well, he went on talking for a long time. He wore us out! It seemed as if he would never end. When the pie – mushroom – was served, Sergey Mikhaylovich took a piece for himself and said, automatically, without thinking, "Hold your tongue and eat your pie." He meant nothing at all by it, of course, but our host took it personally and immediately fell silent. How awkward it was!

MARYA VASSILIYEVNA: *(With a loud laugh.)* So I should imagine!

SEREBRYAKOV: Afterwards, we had a good laugh about it.

VOYNITSKY: *(Aside.)* Yes, very funny!

(Pause.)

SONYA: We've missed you, Godfather. Without you, the winter was so boring. Awful.

ORLOVSKY: Well, my darling, it's time you found a husband.

VOYNITSKY: Sonya? Don't be silly. Where could she find one? Humboldt is dead, so is Schopenhauer, and Edison is in America...The other day she left her diary out on the table. A thing this big! I opened it and this is what I read: "I will never fall in love. Never! Love is egotism, the selfish attraction of my ego to an object of the opposite sex." God knows what she has in there! "Transcendentalism," "the apotheosis of harmonious origins"...whew! Where did you learn all that?

SONYA: Others may tease me, Uncle Zhorzh, but not you.

VOYNITSKY: What's the matter with you?

SONYA: If you say one more word, then one of us will have to go home, you or I!

ORLOVSKY: *(Roaring with laughter.)* What a temper!

VOYNITSKY: Yes, a temper, I'll say! *(To Sonya.)* Come on, paw, please. *(He reaches for her hand.)* Give me your little paw. *(He kisses her hand.)* Peace and harmony! I'll be good.

(Mikhail Lvovich Khrushchov enters from the house.)

KHRUSHCHOV: Oh, if I were only an artist! What a tableau!

ORLOVSKY: Misha! My dear godchild!

KHRUSHCHOV: So Leonid is born! What a day! Hello, Yulichka! How pretty you look! Godfather dear! *(They kiss.)* Sofya Aleksandrovna! *(He exchanges greetings with all.)*

ZHELTOUKHIN: Why are you so late? Where were you?

KHRUSHCHOV: With a patient.

YULYA: The pie is already cold.

KHRUSHCHOV: That's all right, Yulichka, I'll eat it cold! Where do you want me?

SONYA: Sit here. *(She motions to the chair beside her.)*

KHRUSHCHOV: It's a beautiful day and I'm ravenous...a little vodka...*(He pours and drinks.)*...Happy birthday! I'll chase it down with a bite of pie...Yulichka, kiss the pie and make it better! *(She kisses it.)* Merci! So how are things with you, Godfather? It's been a long time...

ORLOVSKY: Yes, it's been quite a while since I've seen you. I've been out of the country, you know.

KHRUSHCHOV: That's what I heard, and I envied you. And how are you, Fyodor?

FYODOR IVANOVICH: Not too bad. We depend upon your prayers.

KHRUSHCHOV: And how's business?

FYODOR IVANOVICH: I can't complain. We're surviving. Only, I'm exhausted, my dear friend! Too much travelling! From here to the Caucasus, from the Caucasus back here, then back to the Caucasus, *et cetera, et cetera,* eternally. I run around like a man possessed. Don't forget, I have two estates there.

KHRUSHCHOV: Yes, I know.

FYODOR IVANOVICH: I busy myself with my colonies, and with catching scorpions and tarantulas. Things in general are all right, but as for "Be still ye tempests of passion!" – all is calm.

KHRUSHCHOV: But you must be in love.

FYODOR IVANOVICH: Wood Demon, that calls for a drink. *(He drinks.)* Gentlemen, never fall in love with married women! Word of honor, it is better to be wounded in the shoulder and shot through the leg, as your poor friend has been, than to love a married woman! It is such a calamity that it is almost...

SONYA: Hopeless?

FYODOR IVANOVICH: What? Hopeless...There is nothing in this world that is hopeless! Hopeless! Star-crossed lovers! Ooh! Ahh! All that is silly. Desire alone is enough. If I want my bullet to hit its mark, then it will! If I want a pretty woman to love me, then she will. That's how it is, brother Sonya! All I need to do is to set my sights on a woman, and it will be easier for her to jump to the moon than to escape me.

SONYA: You're really frightening!

FYODOR IVANOVICH: No one can escape me. No one! Before I could say three sentences to her, she was already in my power...Yes...All I said was: "*Madame,* every time you look at a window, you must think of me. That's what I want." Consequently, she thinks of me a thousand times a day. And on top of that, I bombard her with letters.

YELENA ANDREYEVNA: Letters – not too reliable. She may receive them, but she may not read them.

FYODOR IVANOVICH: You think so? Hmmmm! I have lived on this earth for thirty-five years, and somehow I have never met such a phenomenon, a woman with the courage not to unseal a letter.

Act I

SEREBRYAKOV: Is it interesting?

MARYA VASSILIYEVNA: Interesting, but...strange. He refutes what he himself proposed seven years ago. This is very typical of our times. Never before have people changed their convictions with so little compunction. It's awful!

VOYNITSKY: There's nothing awful about it. Finish your carp, Mother.

MARYA VASSILIYEVNA: But I want to talk!

VOYNITSKY: But we have been talking for the past fifty years about all these various trends and schools of thought. Isn't it time we stopped?

MARYA VASSILIYEVNA: For some reason, you can't stand hearing me talk. Pardon me, Zhorzh, but you've changed so much this past year that I don't even know you any more. You were a man with firm convictions, an enlightened man...

VOYNITSKY: Ah, yes! An enlightened man who shed nothing but darkness! Allow me to get up...Me, enlightened!...What a cruel joke! I am forty-seven years old, and until last year, I, too, tried to delude myself, as you do, with assorted projects and theories, with the single goal of not seeing the world as it really is. I thought I was doing the right thing. Now I realize how stupid it was to have wasted all those years when I could have had everything that old age now denies me.

SEREBRYAKOV: Just a moment, Zhorzh. You seem to be putting the blame on your former convictions.

SONYA: That's enough, Papa! Not again!

SEREBRYAKOV: Just a moment! You seem to be putting the blame on your former convictions. The fault is not in them, however, but in you. You have forgotten that convictions are useless without actions. You should have done things!

VOYNITSKY: Done things? Not everyone can be a *perpetuum mobile*.

SEREBRYAKOV: What do you mean by that?

VOYNITSKY: Nothing. Let's end this conversation. We're not at home.

MARYA VASSILIYEVNA: What am I thinking of? I forgot to remind you, Aleksander, you're supposed to take your drops before lunch! I brought them with me, but I forgot to remind you...

SEREBRYAKOV: I don't want them.

MARYA VASSILIYEVNA: But you're sick, Aleksander, very sick!

SEREBRYAKOV: Well, ring the bells and make a proclamation! Old, ill, old, ill! That's all I ever hear. Leonid Stepanovich, allow me to go inside. It's too hot out here, and the mosquitoes are beginning to bite.

ZHELTOUKHIN: Please, of course! We're finished.

SEREBRYAKOV: I thank you. *(He goes into the house. Marya Vassiliyevna follows him.)*

YULYA: *(To her brother.)* Go in with the professor. It's only polite.

ZHELTOUKHIN: The hell with him. *(He leaves.)*

DYADIN: Yuliya Stepanovna, allow me to thank you from the bottom of my heart. *(He kisses her hand.)*

YULYA: For what, Ilya Ilyich? You ate so little! *(All thank her.)* You're welcome, you're welcome, dear friends, you've hardly touched anything.

FYODOR IVANOVICH: So what's next? Let's go settle our croquet bet...and then what?

YULYA: And then we'll have dinner.

FYODOR IVANOVICH: And after that?

KHRUSHCHOV: After that, come over to my house. We'll go fishing on the lake.

Act I

FYODOR IVANOVICH: Excellent!

DYADIN: Delightful!

SONYA: Now let's see...first, we'll settle our bet...then we'll have an early dinner here at Yulya's...and then around seven we'll go to the Wood De...to Mikhail Lvovich's house. Perfect. Yulichka, let's get the balls and mallets. *(She and Yulya exit into the house.)*

FYODOR IVANOVICH: Vassili, bring the wine to the wickets. We'll drink to the health of the victors. Well, come along, Pater, and join us in the sport of kings.

ORLOVSKY: Wait for me, dear heart, I have to talk to the Professor for five minutes or so, to be polite. Etiquette demands it. Play my ball until I get there! *(As he exits into the house.)* I'll be...soon...

DYADIN: Now I, too, in keen anticipation of the loftiest delights, will go in to listen to the most learned Aleksander Vladimirovich...

VOYNITSKY: Boring, Waffles! Go, go!

DYADIN: I'm off! *(He exits into the house.)*

FYODOR IVANOVICH: *(Singing, as he goes off into the garden.)* "And you, my best and truest friend,/Shall be the queen of all that is."

KHRUSHCHOV: Now I really do have to go. Yegor Petrovich, please, I beg of you, let's not ever talk any more about either forests or medicine. I don't know why, but whenever you begin a discussion about either subject, I have a bad taste in my mouth the rest of the day. And now, I must say good-by. *(He exits.)*

VOYNITSKY: What a narrow-minded fool! Anyone can say foolish things occasionally, but I just can't stand when they are said with such absurd heroics.

YELENA ANDREYEVNA: Once again, Zhorzh, your behavior is impossible. Did you have to quarrel with Marya Vassiliyevna and with Aleksander, and talk about a *perpetuum mobile!* How stupid!

VOYNITSKY: And if I despise him!

YELENA ANDREYEVNA: There's no reason to despise Aleksander. He's no different from anybody else...

(Sonya and Yulya come out with the croquet things and go off into the garden.)

VOYNITSKY: If only you could see yourself, the way you look, the way you move...How lazy you are, and bored with life! Oh, how bored!

YELENA ANDREYEVNA: Lazy and bored, exactly!

(Pause.)

Everyone attacks my husband in front of me, as if it's the most natural thing in the world. Everyone regards me with compassion: poor thing, her husband is old. Everyone wants me to leave Aleksander, even those with the best intentions...This great concern for me, all these compassionate looks and sighs of pity, all come down to the same thing. You heard Wood Demon just now: man rashly destroys the forests, and soon there will be nothing left. In the very same way, men destroy each other, and soon, because of their folly, there will be no more loyalty, or purity, or capacity for self-sacrifice. When someone else's wife is faithful, why can't you men just accept it? How right Wood Demon is! All of you are possessed by the spirit of destruction. You don't care! You don't care about forests, about birds, about women, or even about each other!

VOYNITSKY: I don't like all this philosophy.

YELENA ANDREYEVNA: Tell Fyodor Ivanich that he bores me with his insolence. It's disgusting! In front of everyone, to look me in the eye and proclaim his love for some married woman – what a wit!

(Voices in the garden: "Bravo! Bravo!")

But what a dear man that Wood Demon is. He comes to our house frequently, but I'm shy, and I've never greeted him

Act II

SEREBRYAKOV: What do I want with your Wood Demon? He knows as much about medicine as I do about astronomy!

SONYA: It doesn't require a hospital staff to treat a case of gout.

SEREBRYAKOV: I won't even talk to that fanatic.

SONYA: Do as you please. *(She sits.)* It's up to you.

SEREBRYAKOV: What time is it?

YELENA ANDREYEVNA: Past one.

SEREBRYAKOV: I can't breathe...Sonya, get me my drops. *(She gives him some drops.)* No, not these drops. I can never ask you for anything!

SONYA: Please don't be difficult. Some people may enjoy this behavior, but please, spare me, I don't like it.

SEREBRYAKOV: That girl has such a bad disposition. What makes you act so angry?

SONYA: And what makes you act so miserable? Someone might believe you, when you are actually one of the happiest men in the world.

SEREBRYAKOV: Yes, of course! I am very, very happy!

SONYA: You certainly are!...And if all you have is gout, you know very well that the attack will be over by morning. So what are you moaning about? Such a fuss!

(Voynitsky enters, in a robe, carrying a candle.)

VOYNITSKY: There's going to be a storm. *(A flash of lightning.)* Here it comes! Helène and Sonya, go get some sleep. I've come to relieve you.

SEREBRYAKOV: No, no! Don't leave me alone with him! He'll talk me to death.

VOYNITSKY: But they have to get some rest! They can't sit up with you night after night.

The Wood Demon

SEREBRYAKOV: Then let them go to bed, but you go, too. Thank you, from the bottom of my heart, but I entreat you, in the name of our former friendship, go! We'll talk some other time.

VOYNITSKY: Our "former friendship"...Well, this is news.

YELENA ANDREYEVNA: Don't, Zhorzh.

SEREBRYAKOV: Don't leave me alone with him, my dear! He'll talk me to death.

VOYNITSKY: This is getting to be silly.

KHRUSHCHOV: *(Offstage.)* Are they in the dining room? Please see that my horse is taken care of.

VOYNITSKY: Here's the doctor!

KHRUSHCHOV: *(Entering.)* What a night! The storm was right behind me. I barely made it. Hello. *(He greets everyone.)*

SEREBRYAKOV: I am so sorry they troubled you. I didn't want that at all.

KHRUSHCHOV: Oh, that's all right, it's no trouble. But is this any way to behave, Aleksander Vladimirovich? What's all this fuss about? Shame! Shame on you! This is no good! What seems to be the trouble?

SEREBRYAKOV: Why do doctors speak to their patients in such a condescending way?

KHRUSHCHOV: *(Laughing.)* Because most patients are not so observant! *(Tenderly.)* Well, then, let's get you to bed. You can't be comfortable out here. It'll be warmer in bed, and more restful. Come on...I'll have a look at you, and...all will be well.

YELENA ANDREYEVNA: Do as he says, Sasha. Go on.

KHRUSHCHOV: If it's hard for you to walk, we'll carry you in your chair.

SEREBRYAKOV: No, I'm all right...I can walk...*(He gets up.)*

Act II

But they troubled you for nothing. (*Crossing, with the help of Khrushchov and Sonya.*) I don't have too much faith in... pharmacies. Why are you helping me? I can walk by myself. (*He leaves, with Khrushchov and Sonya.*)

YELENA ANDREYEVNA: He's wearing me out. I'm ready to fall down.

VOYNITSKY: He's wearing you out, and I'm wearing myself out. For three nights now I haven't had any sleep.

YELENA ANDREYEVNA: This is not a happy home. Your mother hates everything except her pamphlets and the professor. The professor is bad-tempered, doesn't trust me, and is afraid of you. Sonya is angry at her father and hardly speaks to me. You despise my husband and show open contempt for your own mother. And I, I'm so tiresome, and irritable, and twenty times today I was on the verge of tears. To be precise, it's a constant battle. What is the meaning of all this? Where is it leading us?

VOYNITSKY: Let's not philosophize.

YELENA ANDREYEVNA: This is not a happy home. You're an educated man, Zhorzh, an intelligent man, and it seems to me that you of all people should understand that it's not the bad people, criminals and traitors, who are ruining the world – it's the hostility between good people, it's secret envy, it's all the little cares and worries which are never seen by those who consider our house a kind of intellectual haven. Help me to reconcile us all. I'm too weak to do it alone.

VOYNITSKY: First, reconcile me with myself! My darling...(*He tries to kiss her hand.*)

YELENA ANDREYEVNA: Stop it! (*She pulls her hand away.*) Go!

VOYNITSKY: Soon the rain will stop, and all of nature will be refreshed and breathe more freely. Only I receive no blessing from the passing storm. Day and night I twist and turn, like a ghost trapped in a house, suffocating with the thought that my life is over. The past is gone, foolishly thrown away, and the present is unbearable, absurd. I offer you my life and my love: what else shall I do with them? What else are they for? My feelings are being wasted, like rays of sunlight in a ditch; and I myself am being wasted.

YELENA ANDREYEVNA: Whenever you talk about love, I begin to feel numb, and I don't know what to say. Forgive me, but I have nothing to say to you. *(She turns to go.)* Good night!

VOYNITSKY: *(Blocking her way.)* If you only knew how I suffer at the thought that right beside me in this very house another life is being wasted – yours. What are you waiting for? What perverse philosophy holds you back? Try to understand that it's not the highest morality to imprison your youth or stifle your lust for life…

YELENA ANDREYEVNA: *(Looking him straight in the eye.)* You're drunk, Zhorzh!

VOYNITSKY: It's possible, it's possible…

YELENA ANDREYEVNA: Is Fyodor Ivanovich still with you?

VOYNITSKY: He's spending the night. It's possible, it's possible. Anything is possible!

YELENA ANDREYEVNA: You've been drinking again all day, haven't you? Why?

VOYNITSKY: Because it gives me the feeling that I'm alive…Don't interfere, Hélène.

YELENA ANDREYEVNA: You never used to drink like this, and you never talked so much. Go to bed. I'm bored with you. And tell your friend Fyodor Ivanovich that if he keeps making a pest of himself, I'll know how to stop him. Now go!

VOYNITSKY: *(Seizing and kissing her hand.)* My darling! My angel!

(Khrushchov comes in.)

KHRUSHCHOV: Yelena Andreyevna, Aleksander Vladimirovich is asking for you.

YELENA ANDREYEVNA: *(Pulling away from Voynitsky.)* Thank

Act II

YELENA ANDREYEVNA: Don't tap. The master is not well.

THE VOICE OF THE WATCHMAN: I'm going. *(He whistles.)* Zhuchka! Trezor! Zhuchka!

(Pause.)

SONYA: *(Returning.)* No.

CURTAIN

ACT THREE

The Serebryakov's living room. Three doors, right, left, and center. Daytime. From offstage, we can hear Yelena Andreyevna playing, on a grand piano, Lenski's aria before the duel in "Evgeny Onegin." Orlovsky, Voynitsky and Fyodor Ivanovich, the latter in a black suit, holding a tall, fur Cossack hat.

VOYNITSKY: *(Listening to the music.)* She's playing, Yelena Andreyevna...My favorite melody. *(The music stops.)* Yes...a fine piece...I think we've probably never been as bored as this...

FYODOR IVANOVICH: You've never known real boredom, my friend. When I volunteered for duty in Serbia, that was real boredom: hot, stifling, dirty... always hung over, my head splitting...I remember sitting once in a dirty little hut...with me, a Captain Kashkinazy. We had run out of things to talk about. Nowhere to go, nothing to do, didn't feel like drinking – so wracked with boredom, you know, that we might just as well have put our heads in a noose. There we were, sitting like cobras, staring at each other...He stares at me, I stare at him...He at me, I at him...So there we were, staring at each other, for no apparent reason...An hour goes by, another, and we're still staring. Suddenly, he jumps up – out of the blue – draws his sword, and comes at me...All rightie! So I whip out mine, of course – or he'll kill me – and we're off! Chik-chak, chik-chak, chik-chak...It took considerable effort to separate us. I came out of it all right, but Captain Kashkinazy still walks around with a scar on his cheek. So, that's how crazy people can get.

ORLOVSKY: Yes, it happens.

(Sonya enters.)

SONYA: *(To herself.)* I don't know what to do with myself! *(She*

Act III

left door.)

YULYA: *(Alone, after a pause.)* Fedyinka's dressed like a cossack...His parents didn't bring him up right...He's the handsomest man in the district, bright, plenty of money, but he'll never amount to anything...He's a prize fool.

(Sonya enters.)

SONYA: Yulichka! I didn't know you were here...

YULYA: *(Kissing her.)* Sonichka.

SONYA: What are you doing? Working? What a fine little manager you are! How I envy you!...You'd make such a good wife. Yulichka, why don't you get married?

YULYA: I don't know...I've had proposals, but I turned them down. The man I'd pick would never want me. *(She sighs.)* Never!

SONYA: What makes you say that?

YULYA: I haven't had much education. In my second year, they took me out of school.

SONYA: Why, Yulichka?

YULYA: I wasn't good at it.

(Sonya laughs.)

Why are you laughing, Sonichka?

SONYA: I don't know – everything seems so strange to me today, Yulichka... I'm so happy, so happy, that it's wearing me out...I don't know what to do with myself! ...Well, what shall we talk about?...Have you ever been in love? *(Yulya nods.)* Yes? *(Yulya nods.)* Is he handsome? *(Yulya whispers in her ear.)* W h o ? Fyodor Ivanich?

YULYA: *(Nodding.)* What about you?

SONYA: Me, too...But it's not Fyodor Ivanich. *(She laughs.)*

Well, tell me more.

YULYA: I've wanted to talk to you for such a long time, Sonichka.

SONYA: Go ahead.

YULYA: I want to explain something. You see...I have always felt very close to you...Of all the girls I know, I like you the very best... If you should say to me, "Yulichka, give me ten horses," or, let's say, "two hundred sheep," I'd say, "Gladly!" I'd never deny you anything...

SONYA: What's wrong, Yulichka? What's the matter?

YULYA: I'm embarrassed...I...I feel so close to you. You're the best of all...You're not proud...And what a pretty little dress that is!

SONYA: We'll talk about dresses later...Tell me...

YULYA: I don't know how to say it cleverly...Allow me to suggest to you...for the sake of happiness...I mean...I mean...I mean...Marry Lyonichka! *(She hides her face in her hands.)*

SONYA: *(Rising.)* Let's not talk about this, Yulichka...No, don't...

(Yelena Andreyevna enters.)

YELENA ANDREYEVNA: There's no privacy in this house. The two Orlovskys and Zhorzh just keep walking around, one room after another. Wherever I go, there they are. It's too much! What are they doing here? Let them go someplace else.

YULYA: *(Tearfully.)* Hello, Yelena Andreyevna. *(Yulya moves to kiss her.)*

YELENA ANDREYEVNA: Hello, Yulichka. Forgive me, I don't like all this kissing. Where's your father, Sonya?

(Pause.)

Sonya, why don't you answer me? I asked you where your

Act III

father is.

(Pause.)

Sonya, why don't you answer?

SONYA: Do you really want to know? Come here...*(She takes her aside.)* I'll tell you, if you insist...My heart is too full to talk to you, Yelena Andryevna, without being completely honest. I think this is yours. *(She hands her a letter.)* I found it in the garden....Let's go, Yulichka! *(She and Yulya exit through the left door.)*

YELENA ANDREYEVNA: *(Alone.)* What's this? A letter to me – from Zhorzh! But what have I done? Oh, how uncharitable! How cruel!...Her heart is so full she can't even talk to me...My God, what an insult!...My head is spinning. I'm going to faint...

(Fyodor Ivanovich enters from the door on the left and crosses the stage.)

FYODOR IVANOVICH: Why do you always jump when you see me?

(Pause.)

Hmmm!...*(He takes the letter out of her hands and tears it into little pieces.)* Stop all this nonsense...You must think only of me.

(Pause.)

YELENA ANDREYEVNA: What does this mean?

FYODOR IVANOVICH: This means that when I set my sights on a woman, she can't escape me.

YELENA ANDREYEVNA: No, it means that you are stupid and insolent!

FYODOR IVANOVICH: This evening, at seven-thirty, on the little bridge behind the garden, I want you to be waiting for me...Well? That's all I have to say...And so, my angel, till seven-thirty. *(He tries to take her hand. She slaps him.)* Forcefully put.

The Wood Demon

YELENA ANDREYEVNA: Get away from me.

FYODOR IVANOVICH: Of course...(*He moves away, then returns.*) I'm touched...Let's discuss this calmly. You see...I've done everything. There's nothing in the world I haven't tried. I've even had goldfish soup, once or twice...but I've never yet gone up in a balloon, and I've never stolen any wives from illustrious professors...

YELENA ANDREYEVNA: Go away.

FYODOR IVANOVICH: I'm going...I've done everything ...That's why I'm so arrogant it's...staggering...What I mean is...I'm saying all this because...if you ever need a friend, or a faithful hound, you can always turn to me...I am so touched by this!

YELENA ANDREYEVNA: I don't need any hounds...Go away...

FYODOR IVANOVICH: Of course. (*Deeply moved.*) And yet, I'm touched...yes, deeply touched. Yes...(*He goes off uncertainly.*)

YELENA ANDREYEVNA: (*Alone.*) My head aches...Every night I have bad dreams. I have a feeling something terrible is going to happen...How vile! These young people were born and brought up together, they are all intimate friends, always kissing. They should be living in peace and harmony, but instead they may soon eat each other up...Wood Demon tries to save the forests, but who is there to save the people? (*She goes to the door at the left, but sees Zheltoukhin and Yulya approaching. She turns and exits through the center door.*)

YULYA: (*Entering with Zheltoukhin.*) How unlucky we are, Lyonichka! Oh, how unlucky!

ZHELTOUKHIN: Who commissioned you to speak to her? Who asked you to play the village matchmaker? You've ruined everything. She'll think I can't speak for myself...and what a common thing to do! A thousand times I've told you to forget it. No good can come of it, nothing but humiliation and all sorts of innuendos, deceptions, and ugliness...The old man probably realizes that I'm in love with her and is trying to take advantage of it! He wants me to buy this estate.

Act III

VOYNITSKY: For twenty-five years I have managed this estate. I worked, I sent you money like the most faithful steward, and in all this time you have never once thanked me. All this time – from when I was young until this very day – you have paid me five hundred rubles a year – a beggarly wage! And never once has it occurred to you to raise that wage by a single ruble.

SEREBRYAKOV: Zhorzh, how could I know?...I'm not a practical man. I don't understand these things. You could have raised your own wages as much as you liked.

VOYNITSKY: You mean, why didn't I steal? Do all of you think I'm a fool because I didn't steal? I should have – it would have been only fair – and I wouldn't be such a poor man today!

MARYA VASSILIYEVNA: Zhorzh!

DYADIN: *(Agitated.)* Zhorzhinka, don't, don't...I'm trembling ...Why destroy such good relations? *(He kisses him.)* Don't...

VOYNITSKY: For twenty-five years, I've been here with her, with this old mother of mine - sitting like a mole inside these four walls. All our thoughts and feelings belonged to you. In the daytime, we talked only about you and your works, we were so proud of you, we shared in your glory, we never spoke your name without reverence. And we squandered every night reading your books and articles, all of which I now despise with all my being.

DYADIN: Zhorzhinka, don't...I can't...

SEREBRYAKOV: I don't understand this – what do you want from me?

VOYNITSKY: To us, you were a superior being, and we read each new article until we knew it by heart...How blind I was! But now, everything is clear! You write about art, but you don't know anything about art! And all your work that I loved so much is not worth half a kopeck.

SEREBRYAKOV: Stop him! Can't anyone make him stop? Or I'll leave.

YELENA ANDREYEVNA: Zhorzh, I insist that you shut up! Do you hear me?

VOYNITSKY: I won't shut up. *(He blocks Serebryakov's way.)* Wait, I haven't finished! You have ruined my life! I haven't lived! I haven't lived! Thanks to you, I have wasted the best years of my life! You are my worst enemy!

DYADIN: I can't...I can't...I'll be in the drawing room! *(He goes out in great agitation.)*

SEREBRYAKOV: What do you want from me? And what right do you have to speak to me in this tone of voice. You nobody! If the estate is yours, then take it. I have no need of it.

ZHELTOUKHIN: What a stew! I'm leaving! *(He goes out.)*

YELENA ANDREYEVNA: If you don't shut up, I'll leave this inferno this very instant. *(Shouting.)* I can't take any more of this!

VOYNITSKY: My life is over! I'm a man of intelligence, ability, courage. If I had lived a normal life, I could have been a Schopenhauer, a Dostoevsky...What am I babbling about? I must be losing my mind...Mother! Mother, help me!

MARYA VASSILIYEVNA: Obey the professor!

VOYNITSKY: Mother! What shall I do? No, no, don't tell me! I know exactly what to do! *(To Serebryakov)* You will remember me! *(He leaves through the center door. Marya Vassiliyevna follows him out.)*

SEREBRYAKOV: Ladies and gentlemen, what is this all about? Keep that maniac away from me!

ORLOVSKY: It's all right, it's all right, Sasha. Let him be. He'll find peace. Give him time. Don't upset yourself.

SEREBRYAKOV: I can't live under the same roof with him. He lives here *(He points to the center door.)*, almost on top of me...Let him move to the village, or to another wing. Or I will have to move. I won't go on living with him...

Act III

YELENA ANDREYEVNA: If anything like this ever happens again, I'm leaving.

SEREBRYAKOV: Oh, please, don't try to frighten me.

YELENA ANDREYEVNA: I'm not trying to frighten you, but all of you seem to be conspiring to make my life a hell on earth...I'll go!

SEREBRYAKOV: Everybody knows perfectly well that you're young and I'm old, and that you are doing me a big favor by living here...

YELENA ANDREYEVNA: Go on, go on...

ORLOVSKY: Now, now, now...My friends!...

(Khrushchov enters quickly.)

KHRUSHCHOV: *(With emotion.)* I am very happy to find you at home, Aleksander Vladimirovich...Forgive me, perhaps I've come at a bad time. I hope I'm not disturbing you...but that's beside the point. Hello...

SEREBRYAKOV: What do you want?

KHRUSHCHOV: Excuse me, I need to catch my breath – I rode over here so fast...Aleksander Vladimirovich, I just heard that you sold your forest a few days ago to Kuznetsov, for timber. If this is true, and not just a rumor, then I beg you not to do it.

YELENA ANDREYEVNA: Mikhail Lvovich, my husband is in no mood to talk business. Come with me into the garden.

KHRUSHCHOV: I must speak to him right now!

YELENA ANDREYEVNA: Do as you like...I can't...*(She exits.)*

KHRUSHCHOV: Let me go to Kuznetsov and tell him that you've changed your mind...May I? Will you let me do that? To cut down a thousand trees, to destroy them, for two or three thousand rubles, for a few whims, fancy clothes, luxuries...to destroy them, so that future generations will condemn us as barbarians! If you, a learned, famous man, can decide to do such a heartless thing, then what will the simple people do? It's appalling.

ORLOVSKY: Later, Misha, not now.

SEREBRYAKOV: Let's go, Ivan Ivanovich, this will never end. (*Khrushchov blocks his way.*)

KHRUSHCHOV: If that's the way you feel, Professor, then listen to this. Wait! I have some money coming. In three months, I'll buy it from you myself.

ORLOVSKY: Excuse me, Misha, but this doesn't make sense …All right, let's say you are a man of ideals…we're grateful for that, we bow to you (*He makes a low bow.*), but why tear the house down?

KHRUSHCHOV: (*Angrily.*) Universal Godfather! There are so many agreeable people in the world, but I'm always suspicious of them. They "agree" about everything only because they don't care enough – about anything – to disagree!

ORLOVSKY: I can see you came here to pick a fight, my dear…Shame on you! Ideas are ideas, brother, but you have to have this thing, too. (*He points to his heart.*)…Without this thing, my soul, all your forests and all your peat aren't worth half a kopeck…Now don't take this too hard, but you are still so young, oh, such a boy.

SEREBRYAKOV: (*Sharply.*) And next time, be so good as to have yourself announced. And please spare me such a psychopathic display in the future. Well, you all wanted me to lose my temper, and now you've accomplished it! Be so good as to leave me! All your forests and your peat bogs…as far as I'm concerned…psychopathic! Sheer, raving fanaticism! That is my opinion. Come, Ivan Ivanovich. (*He leaves.*)

ORLOVSKY: (*Following him.*) Sasha, you've gone too far…Why be so hard on him? (*He leaves.*)

KHRUSHCHOV: (*Alone, after a pause.*) Psychopathic, fanaticism. In other words, in the opinion of the illustrious professor, I'm mad…well, I humbly bend to the authority of your imperial wisdom, and I am going straight home to shave my head! No, it's the earth that's mad, for preserving you. *(He goes quickly to the door at the right. Sonya enters from the door at the left, where she has been listening since Khrushchov's arrival.)*

SONYA: *(Running after him.)* Wait!...I heard everything...Say something... Say something quickly. Unless you do, I will have to! I can't stand this any longer!

KHRUSHCHOV: Sofya Aleksandrovna, everything I had to say, I said. I begged your father to spare the forest, and I was right! But he insulted me, called me a madman. Me, mad!

SONYA: Stop, stop...

KHRUSHCHOV: Oh, yes, those who disguise their heartlessness as learning, their lack of soul as wisdom, they're not mad! And they're not mad who marry old men just to deceive them in front of everyone, and just so they can buy the latest fashions with the profits they get from the criminal destruction of the forests!

SONYA: Listen to me, listen...*(She takes his hands and holds them tightly.)* Let me tell you...

KHRUSHCHOV: That's enough. Let's end this. I'm a stranger to you. I already know your opinion of me. There's nothing else for me to do here. That's it. I'm sorry that our brief acquaintance – which I treasured – will only leave me with the memory of your father's gout and your critique of my liberal sympathies...But it's not my fault...not mine...*(Sonya covers her face with her hands and goes quickly through the door at the left.)* I should never have fallen in love here. Well, that'll teach me. Get me out of this place! *(He goes toward the door at the right.)*

(Yelena Andreyevna enters from the door at the left.)

YELENA ANDREYEVNA: You're still here! Don't go...Ivan Ivanovich just told me that my husband was rude to you...I'm so sorry, he is in a bad mood today and doesn't understand you. As for me, Mikhail Lvovich, my heart is on your side. I have so much respect for you. I am so moved. Allow me, with all my heart, to offer you my friendship. *(She extends both hands to him.)*

KHRUSHCHOV: *(With distaste)* Get away from me...I despise your friendship. *(He exits.)*

YELENA ANDREYEVNA: *(Alone, grieving.)* Why? Why?

(A shot is heard. Marya Vassiliyevna enters, unsteadily, from the center door. She gives a scream and faints. Sonya enters left and runs out center. Serebryakov, Orlovsky and Zheltoukhin enter. Cries of "What is it?," etc. Offstage, Sonya screams, then comes in again.)

SONYA: *(Screaming.)* Uncle Zhorzh has shot himself! *(She runs back out. Orlovsky, Serebryakov and Zheltoukhin follow her.)*

YELENA ANDREYEVNA: Why? Why?

(Dyadin enters through the door at the right.)

DYADIN: *(In the doorway.)* What is it?

YELENA ANDREYEVNA: Take me away! Cast me into the deepest pit – do away with me! – but I cannot stay here any longer! Quickly, I beseech you! *(She leaves with Dyadin.)*

CURTAIN

ACT FOUR

The forest. The house by the water-mill, which Dyadin rents from Khrushchov. Yelena Andreyevna and Dyadin are sitting on a bench under the window.

YELENA ANDREYEVNA: Ilya Ilyich, my dear, will you go to the post office again tomorrow?

DYADIN: *Absolument.*

YELENA ANDREYEVNA: I'll wait another three days. If my brother doesn't send me an answer, I'll borrow some money from you and go to Moscow. After all, I can't stay with you here at the mill for a hundred years.

DYADIN: That's a certainty...

(Pause.)

I do not presume to instruct you, and I say this only with the greatest respect, but all your letters and telegrams, and me riding off to the post office every day – all that bustle, forgive me, is useless. Because no matter what answer your brother sends, you will go back to your husband.

YELENA ANDREYEVNA: I won't go back...Let's be logical, Ilya Ilyich. I do not love my husband. I did love the others, but they have never been fair to me. Why should I go back? You'll say it's my duty. I know that perfectly well myself, but I repeat: we must be logical!

(Pause.)

DYADIN: Hmm...The greatest of Russian poets, Lomonosov, fled the province of Archangelsk to seek his destiny in Moscow.

That was as it should be...But why did you flee? If we must be absolutely logical, you don't have a "destiny." The lot of a canary is to sit in a cage and peep out at the happiness of others, even for a hundred years. So, sit!

YELENA ANDREYEVNA: And what if I'm not a canary, but a sparrow, free to fly where I please!

DYADIN: Oh, ho! A bird is recognized by its flight, gracious lady...In the two weeks you've been here, another lady would have had time to visit ten cities, and throw dust in everyone's eyes, but you have only managed to fly as far as the mill, and even that has been more than your little heart can bear...No, no, my dear one. You'll stay with me a little longer, your little heart will recover, and then - you'll go back to your husband. *(He listens.)* There's a carriage coming! *(He rises.)*

YELENA ANDREYEVNA: I'll go.

DYADIN: I will not presume to weary you any longer with my company. I'll go to the mill and have a nap...I got up today before Aurora.

YELENA ANDREYEVNA: When you wake up, come and have tea with me. *(She goes into the house.)*

DYADIN: *(Alone.)* If I moved in intellectual circles, they might very well have drawn up a caricature of me in a journal, with a most amusing, satirical caption. For goodness' sake, in spite of my years and my unattractive appearance, I have stolen the young wife of an illustrious professor! This is delightful! *(He exits.)*

(Semyon enters, carrying pails. Yulya enters.)

YULYA: Hello, Syenka. God be with you! Is Ilya Ilyich at home?

SEMYON: Home. Went to the mill.

YULYA: Call him for me.

SEMYON: I will. *(He exits.)*

YULYA: *(Alone.)* He must be sleeping...*(She sits on the bench under the window and sighs deeply.)* Some sleep, others stroll about, and all I do is work like a dog, day after day...I wish I were dead. *(She sighs even more deeply.)* Dear Lord, how can anybody be as stupid as Waffles? I rode by his barn just now, and a little black pig walked out. When his pigs get into the mill and tear up all the grain sacks, that will teach him a lesson.

(Dyadin enters, putting on his jacket.)

DYADIN: Ah, is that you, Yuliya Stepanovna? Excuse my *déshabillé.* I'm not dressed to receive you...I wanted to rest a while in the arms of Morpheus.

YULYA: Hello, Ilya Ilyich.

DYADIN: Forgive me for not asking you in...Everything is in disarray, and so forth...Come to the mill, if you like...

YULYA: No, this is fine. Let me tell you why I'm here, Ilya Ilyich. Lyonichka and the professor thought of having a picnic today at your mill.

DYADIN: How nice!

YULYA: I came ahead...They'll be here soon. Please have a table brought out, and a samovar, of course...I have everything else. Tell Syenka to bring the baskets from my carriage.

DYADIN: Of course.

(Pause.)

Well, how is everything at your place?

YULYA: Not good...Can you believe it, Ilya Ilyich? So many cares and worries I'm ready to drop! We have the professor and Sonichka living at our house now, you know.

DYADIN: I know.

YULYA: Since Yegor Petrovich did away with himself, they can't stand to be in their own house...They're afraid. It's not too bad in the daylight, but as soon as evening comes, they all get together in one room and sit there till dawn. They're all so frightened of the darkness, frightened that Yegor Petrovich might appear...

DYADIN: Superstition! And do they ever think of Yelena Andreyevna?

YULYA: Of course they do!

(Pause.)

She just disappeared!

DYADIN: It's a subject worthy of the brush of Aivazovsky! ... Disappeared!

YULYA: And we still don't have any idea where she is...Maybe she went somewhere, or maybe, in despair...

DYADIN: The Lord is merciful, Yuliya Stepanovna. All will be well!

(Khrushchov enters with a portfolio and a wooden box of painting materials.)

KHRUSHCHOV: Hello! Anybody home? Semyon!

DYADIN: Look over here!

KHRUSHCHOV: Ah...Hello, Yulichka!

YULYA: Hello, Mikhail Lvovich!

KHRUSHCHOV: Well, here I am again, Ilya Ilyich, to try and get some work done. I just can't sit home any longer. Have my table set up as you did yesterday, under this tree. And have them bring a couple of lamps – it'll be dark soon.

DYADIN: At your service, Your Highness! (He exits.)

KHRUSHCHOV: How are you, Yulichka?

YULYA: So-so...

(Pause.)

Act IV

KHRUSHCHOV: The Serebryakovs are living with you?

YULYA: With us.

KHRUSHCHOV: Hmm – And your Lyonichka, what is he doing?

YULYA: He sits at home...with Sonichka.

KHRUSHCHOV: Of course he does! Why not?

(Pause.)

He ought to marry her.

YULYA: Oh, yes (She sighs.), please God! He's a fine man, with a good education. She comes from a good family, too ... It's what I've always...

KHRUSHCHOV: She's a fool.

YULYA: That's not nice.

KHRUSHCHOV: And your Lyonichka's just like her. What a brain!...They're all the same, everybody over there. A galaxy of wits!

YULYA: You probably missed your lunch.

KHRUSHCHOV: What do you mean?

YULYA: You're so cranky!

(Dyadin and Semyon enter with a middle-sized table.)

DYADIN: Ah, Misha! When you see what you want, you go right for it. What a wonderful spot you've chosen. It's an oasis! A veritable oasis! Let's pretend! Pretend these are all palm trees, Yulichka's a gentle doe, you're a lion, and I'm a tiger.

KHRUSHCHOV: You're a dear man, Ilya Ilyich, a good-hearted man, but what strange ways you have! Each phrase as sweet as sugar candy, clicking your heels, twitching your shoulders... Somebody who didn't know you might think you were a...God knows what – not even human. It's a shame.

DYADIN: And so it is written: that's my nature...Ordained by fate.

KHRUSHCHOV: That's it! "Ordained by fate!" Stop doing that! *(He sets up his work on the table.)* I think I'll spend the night.

DYADIN: That would please me very much!...You're so angry, Misha, but my soul is full of indescribable joy. – It's as if I had a little bird here inside me, singing his song.

KHRUSHCHOV: Be joyful, then.

(Pause.)

You have a little bird in your heart, and I have a toad. Twenty thousand cares and worries. Shimanski sold his forest for timber ...That's one! Yelena Andreyevna ran away from her husband, and now no one knows where she is! That's two! And every day I get more stupid, petty and worthless...That's three! I had something I wanted to tell you yesterday, but I couldn't. – I didn't have the courage! Congratulate me – what a fine man I've turned out to be! The late Yegor Petrovich left a diary, which fell into the hands of Ivan Ivanich, who showed it to me. I read it – about ten times...

YULYA: They read it at our house, too.

KHRUSHCHOV: The affair between Zhorzh and Yelena Andreyevna – which was common knowledge throughout the district – turns out to be nothing but gossip. I believed all those foul, disgusting rumors, and, like everybody else, repeated what I heard. I let myself hate, despise, even insult...

DYADIN: Yes, that's not very nice.

KHRUSHCHOV: The first one I believed, Yulichka, was your brother. Isn't that something! I believed your brother, although I do not respect him, and I did not believe this woman, although she was making every sacrifice, unselfishly, before my very eyes. I'm quicker to think evil than good, and I can't see past the nose on my face, which only proves that I'm as worthless as everybody else.

Act IV

DYADIN: *(To Yulya.)* Come with me to the mill, my child. Let this old crab work by himself. We'll have a nice walk. Come along...Get to work, Misha, my dear. *(They exit.)*

KHRUSHCHOV: *(Alone, diluting his paints in a saucer.)* One night, I saw him press his lips against her hand. The diary gives a full description – of my visit that night, of what I said to him. He quotes my words and calls me a fool...narrow-minded.

(Pause.)

Too thick...It should be lighter. And later, he blames Sonya for falling in love with me...She never loved me...Oops! I've blotched it! ...*(He scrapes the paper with a knife.)* And even if there were any truth in it at all, there's no use dwelling on it. It began foolishly and ended foolishly...

(Semyon and a laborer enter with a large table.)

What's this? What are you doing?

SEMYON: Ilya Ilyich's orders. They're all coming from the Zheltoukhin place for tea.

KHRUSHCHOV: How nice! So much for my work. I'll just have to forget it. I'll just have to pack all this up again and go home.

(Zheltoukhin enters, with Sonya on his arm.)

ZHELTOUKHIN: *(Singing.)* "Against my will, to these sad shores,/Some unknown force compels me..."

KHRUSHCHOV: Who's this? Ah! *(He starts packing quickly.)*

ZHELTOUKHIN: Just one more question, Sophie dear...Do you remember when we were all having lunch on my birthday, and you burst out laughing? You were laughing at me, weren't you, at the way I look?

SONYA: Oh, stop, Leonid Stepanich, how can you say such a thing? I burst out laughing for no reason at all.

ZHELTOUKHIN: Ah, who's this I see? You're here, too? Hello.

KHRUSHCHOV: Hello.

ZHELTOUKHIN: You're working! Good for you! Where is Waffles?

KHRUSHCHOV: There...

ZHELTOUKHIN: Where is "there"?

KHRUSHCHOV: I thought I made it clear...There, at the mill.

ZHELTOUKHIN: I guess I'd better look for him. (*Singing.*) "Against my will, to these sad shores..." (*He goes.*)

SONYA: Hello.

KHRUSHCHOV: Hello.

(*Pause.*)

SONYA: What are you drawing?

KHRUSHCHOV: Oh...nothing, really.

SONYA: A design?

KHRUSHCHOV: No, a map of the forests in our district. I made it myself.

(*Pause.*)

The green is for the places where there were forests in our grandparents' day, and earlier. The light green – where forests have been destroyed in the last twenty-five years. And the blue – where the forests still exist...So...

(*Pause.*)

Well, how about you? Are you happy?

SONYA: This is not the time to think of happiness, Mikhail Lvovich.

KHRUSHCHOV: So what should we think about?

Act IV

SONYA: We thought too much about happiness. It brought us grief.

KHRUSHCHOV: Um-hmm.

(*Pause.*)

SONYA: There's nothing so bad but some good may come of it. Grief has taught me that we should not think about our own happiness, but about the happiness of others. We must sacrifice ourselves, Mikhail Lvovich, all our lives!

KHRUSHCHOV: Well, yes…

(*Pause.*)

Your grandmother's son shot himself, and she's still busy with her pamphlets, looking for "inconsistencies." Fate deals you a blow, and you decide to ruin your life – you call it "sacrifice" – and it makes you feel better…No one is selfless…You're not and I'm not, either…The things we really ought to do, we leave undone, and everything turns to dust and ashes…I'm in the way here. I'll go now, and leave you with Zheltoukhin. What are you crying about? I didn't mean to make you cry.

SONYA: (*Brushing away her tears.*) It's all right, it's nothing…

(*Yulya, Dyadin and Zheltoukhin enter.*)

SEREBRYAKOV: (*Offstage.*) Aou-ooo! Where is everybody?

SONYA: (*Shouting.*) Here, Papa!

DYADIN: Here comes the samovar (*Semyon enters with the samovar. Dyadin fusses at the table, with Yulya.*) How delightful!

(*Serebryakov and Orlovsky enter.*)

SONYA: Over here, Papa!

SEREBRYAKOV: I see, I see.

ZHELTOUKHIN: (*Loudly.*) Ladies and gentlemen, the council is now in session! Waffles, uncork the cherry wine.

KHRUSHCHOV: Professor...can we forget what happened between us? *(He offers his hand.)* I ask your forgiveness...

SEREBRYAKOV: Thank you. I'm glad. You forgive me, too. The day after that incident, when I tried to reflect on everything that happened and remembered our conversation, I felt terrible...Let us be friends. *(He takes Khrushchov by the hand and leads him to the table.)*

ORLOVSKY: It's about time, dear heart. A bad peace is better than a good battle.

DYADIN: Your Excellency, I am so happy that you have found your way to my oasis. Delighted beyond words!

SEREBRYAKOV: I thank you, my esteemed friend. It's beautiful here, an oasis, indeed.

ORLOVSKY: Oh, are you fond of the great outdoors, Sasha?

SEREBRYAKOV: Oh, yes!

(Pause.)

Let's not be silent, ladies and gentlemen – talk. We must talk. In our situation, it's the best thing we can do. We must face our misfortunes bravely, without blinking. And I must be the bravest, because I am the most unhappy.

YULYA: I'm not putting any sugar in the tea. Help yourselves to the jam.

DYADIN: *(Fussing about his guests.)* Oh, I'm so happy! So happy!

SEREBRYAKOV: I've been through so much lately, Mikhail Lvovich, and I've thought so long and hard about everything, that I could probably write a comprehensive treatise for the edification of posterity on how to live. "Live a century, study a century" – but it's adversity that teaches us.

DYADIN: "He who brings back the past should have his eyes put out." God is merciful, and all will be well.

(Sonya shudders.)

Act IV

ZHELTOUKHIN: Why did you jump?

SONYA: Someone cried out.

DYADIN: It must be the peasants, down by the river, catching crayfish.

(Pause.)

ZHELTOUKHIN: I thought we decided to spend this evening as if nothing had happened, my friends...And yet, there's tension in the air...

DYADIN: Your Excellency, my position in regard to learning is not only reverential, but also a kind of kinship. My brother Grigori Ilyich has a wife, who has a brother – perhaps you've heard of him – Konstantin Gavrilich Novosyelov? He holds an advanced degree in Foreign Letters.

SEREBRYAKOV: Well, the name is familiar to me...

(Pause.)

YULYA: It'll be exactly fifteen days tomorrow since Yegor Petrovich died.

KHRUSHCHOV: Let's not talk about it, Yulichka.

SEREBRYAKOV: Courage, do not falter!

(Pause.)

ZHELTOUKHIN: And yet there's still tension in the air...

SEREBRYAKOV: Nature abhors a vacuum. Two dear ones have been taken away from me, and new friends have already been sent to fill the void. I drink to your health, Leonid Stepanovich!

ZHELTOUKHIN: I thank you, dear Aleksander Vladimirovich! But first, let me offer a toast to your many academic achievements:
Sow the seeds of wisdom! Sow!
The seeds of goodness! Let them grow!

The Wood Demon

And the Russian people will thank you!

SEREBRYAKOV: I'm so grateful for these kind words. And I am longing for the day when our friendly relations will grow even closer.

(Fyodor Ivanovich enters.)

FYODOR IVANOVICH: What do we have here, a picnic?

ORLOVSKY: My son! My beauty!

FYODOR IVANOVICH: Greetings, all. *(He kisses Sonya and Yulia.)*

ORLOVSKY: I haven't seen him for two whole weeks. Where were you? What have you been doing?

FYODOR IVANOVICH: I went to Lyonya's. They told me there that you were here – so I came here.

ORLOVSKY: Where have you been gallivanting?

FYODOR IVANOVICH: Haven't slept for three days... Yesterday, later, I dropped five thousand rubles – at cards. Drank, played cards, dashed into town about five times...Went completely crazy.

ORLOVSKY: That's my boy! And aren't you still a little...?

FYODOR IVANOVICH: Steady as a rock. Tea, Yulka – With lemon – lots of it! Well, what do you think about old Zhorzh, uh? Out of the blue click-click-pow! – blows his brains out! And how does he do it. With a French gun, a Lefauché! As if he couldn't lay his hand on a good Smith and Wesson.

KHRUSHCHOV: You stupid ox, shut up!

FYODOR IVANOVICH: An ox? Perhaps, but what a pedigree! *(He runs his fingers through his beard.)* Just think what the beard alone would bring...I may be an ox, a fool, a good for nothing – but all I have to do is will it, and any girl will be my bride. Sonya, marry me! *(To Khrushchov.)* Uh-oh, my mistake. Pardon.

❖ 72 ❖

Act IV

KHRUSHCHOV: What a clown. Enough!

YULYA: There's no hope for you, Fedyinka! You're the biggest drunkard and prodigal son in the district. It makes me sad even to look at you. Sultan of sultans – nothing but trouble!

FYODOR IVANOVICH: Another lamentation. Come and sit by me...That's more like it...I'll come and spend two weeks with you, Yulichka. I need a rest. *(He kisses her.)*

YULYA: Shame on you for behaving this way. You should be a comfort to your father in his old age, instead of a disgrace. What a stupid way to live! Stupid!

FYODOR IVANOVICH: I'll never drink again! *Basta! (He pours himself some wine.)* Is this plum or cherry?

YULYA: What are you doing? Don't drink, then!

FYODOR IVANOVICH: One little glass won't hurt. *(He drinks.)* Take my two horses and my gun, Wood Demon, a gift! I'll be at Yulya's for a couple of weeks.

KHRUSHCHOV: You ought to be confined to quarters.

YULYA: Here, have some tea!

DYADIN: And some biscuits, too, Fedyinka.

ORLOVSKY: O brother Sasha, I led just the same sort of life as my Fyodor until I was forty. One day, my dear, I began to make a list of all the hearts I'd broken in my lifetime. I counted and counted – up to seventy before I stopped! But when I turned forty, something came over me, brother Sasha, a kind of melancholy. I felt lost. In a word, my soul was full of discord. That's how it was. I tried this and that, I read, worked, traveled – and none of it was any use at all. One day, dear heart, I went to visit His Excellency, the late Dmitri Pavlovich...one of his children is a godchild of mine...We had a few drinks, delicacies, dinner...And after dinner, for want of something better to do – we put up a target in the courtyard and did some shooting. A huge crowd gathered, people came from miles around. Our Waffles was there.

DYADIN: I was there, I was there…I remember.

ORLOVSKY: I felt such sadness, you know – My god! I couldn't bear it! And suddenly, tears gushed from my eyes—my head began to spin – and I shouted out with all my might: "Dear friends, good people, forgive me, for the sake of Our Lord Jesus Christ!" And at that very moment, my heart was filled with sweetness and warmth, my soul was cleansed. And from that time to this, dear friend, no happier man could be found in the district. And you must do the same.

SEREBRYAKOV: Do what?

(There is a reddish glow in the sky.)

ORLOVSKY: Just what I did. Capitulate. Open your heart.

SEREBRYAKOV: This is a good example of our native Russian folk-wisdom. You advise me to beg forgiveness. For what? Let them beg my forgiveness!

SONYA: But Papa, we're the guilty ones

SEREBRYAKOV: Is that so? You are probably all thinking of my relations with my wife. Is it really possible that you think I am the guilty one? That's ridiculous. She has betrayed her marriage vows and deserted me at a most difficult time…

KHRUSHCHOV: Let me say something, Aleksander Vladimirovich, and hear me out. For twenty-five years you have been a professor serving Knowledge. I plant forests and practice medicine. But why? For whom are we doing all this if we are not kind to those who depend on us? We say that we serve humanity, and at the same time we destroy each other without mercy. Did we do anything, for example, to save Zhorzh? And where is your wife, whom we have all treated so unjustly? Where is your own peace and tranquility? Where is your daughter's? Everything is ruined, lost, turned to dust…You call me "Wood Demon," but I'm not the only one. There's a "wood demon" lurking in each one of you. You all wander through the dark woods and live by groping. We have just enough imagination, understanding, and tenderness to spoil our own lives and the lives of others.

Act IV

(Yelena Andreyevna comes quietly out of the house and sits on a bench under the window.)

I considered myself an idealist, a lover of mankind, and yet I never forgave the smallest mistake. I believed everything I heard, even spread the gossip myself. And when your wife, for example, generously offered me her friendship, I sneered down at her from my lofty height, "Get away from me! I despise your friendship!" That's the kind of man I am. There is a "wood demon" inside me. I'm just like everybody else...shallow, stupid...But you're no eagle yourself, professor! And, nevertheless, the people in this district – all the women, anyway – see me as a hero – and you, well, you're famous all over Russia. But if a man like me can really be thought of as a hero, and a man like you really regarded as famous, it just means that in such a void any nobody can be a king. There are no true heroes, no men of real ability, there is no one to lead us out of the dark woods, to rebuild what we destroy, there are no true eagles who deserve their glory...

SEREBRYAKOV: I beg your pardon...but I did not come here to engage in polemics with you and justify my right to fame!

ZHELTOUKHIN: All right, Misha, let's end this conversation!

KHRUSHCHOV: I'll be through in a minute, then I'll go. Yes, I'm just like everybody else, a little man – but you're no giant yourself, professor. Zhorzh was a little man, too – his best idea was to blow his brains out. We're all little men! As for the women...

YELENA ANDREYEVNA: *(Interrupting.)* As for the women, they're not much bigger. *(She crosses to the table.)* Yelena Andreyevna has left her husband, and do you think she'll make good use of her freedom? Don't worry...she'll come back...*(She sits down at the table.)* You see, she's back already.

(General confusion.)

DYADIN: *(Roaring with laughter.)* This is delightful! Ladies and gentlemen, don't chop my head off without a hearing! I'm the one who abducted your wife, Your Excellency, just as once upon a time a certain Paris stole away Helen the Fair! I! Although there may be no Parises with pockmarks, friend Horatio, there are more things on earth than our philosophers ever dreamed about!

KHRUSHCHOV: I'm completely lost...Can it be you, Yelena Andreyevna?

YELENA ANDREYEVNA: These past two weeks, I've lived here at Ilya Ilyich's...Why are you all looking at me like that? Well, hello...I've been sitting by the window, and I heard every word. Hello, my dear. *(She embraces Sonya.)* Let's be friends...Peace and harmony.

DYADIN: *(Rubbing his hands together.)* This is delightful!

YELENA ANDREYEVNA: Mikhail Lvovich...*(She offers him her hand.)* "He who brings back the past should have his eyes put out."...Hello, Fyodor Ivanich ...Yulichka...

ORLOVSKY: Our little darling, our very own professor's wife, our beauty!... She has returned! She has come back to us!

YELENA ANDREYEVNA: I missed all of you. Hello, Aleksander! *(She holds out her hand to her husband, but he turns away.)* Aleksander!

SEREBRYAKOV: You have betrayed your marriage vows.

YELENA ANDREYEVNA: Aleksander!

SEREBRYAKOV: Yelena Andreyevna, I won't deny that I am very happy to see you and to speak with you, but not here: at home... *(He walks away from the table.)*

ORLOVSKY: Sasha !

(Pause.)

YELENA ANDREYEVNA: So...This means that our difficulties, Aleksander, are dealt with very simply: not at all. So be it. I'm only a passer-by, my lot is to enjoy the happiness of a canary, of a peasant's wife – to sit at home for a hundred years, to eat, drink, and sleep, and hear, day after day, about gout and rights and proper rewards. Why have you all lowered your eyes? Are you embarrassed? Let's have some wine, shall we? Hurrah!

Act IV

DYADIN: All will be settled, all will be set right, things will get better, and all will be well.

FYODOR IVANOVICH: *(Approaching Serebryakov, with emotion.)* Aleksander Vladimirovich, I am so touched by all this...I implore you, take her to your bosom, just say one kind word to her, and, I give you my solemn promise, I'll be your faithful friend forever and give you my best troika.

SEREBRYAKOV: Thank you, but, forgive me, I do not understand you...

FYODOR IVANOVICH: Hmm...You do not understand... Coming back from a hunt one day, I look up – and there's an enormous owl sitting in a tree...I pop at him with birdshot! He sits...I try number nine shot...Still he sits...Nothing gets through to him. He just sits there, blinking.

SEREBRYAKOV: To what are you referring?

FYODOR IVANOVICH: To an enormous owl. *(He goes back to the table.)*

ORLOVSKY: *(Listening.)* Quiet, please, everybody. I think I hear the alarm.

FYODOR IVANOVICH: *(Seeing the reddish glow in the sky.)*Hey, hey, hey – look at the sky! What a blaze!

ORLOVSKY: Well, well. And here we sat and never noticed!

DYADIN: My, my.

FYODOR IVANOVICH: *(Imitating a bugle.)* Te-te-te! That's some fire. Over by Alekseyevsk!

KHRUSHCHOV: No, Alekseyevsk is further right...It's closer to Novopetrovsk!

YULYA: How awful! I'm afraid of fires!

KHRUSHCHOV: Yes, it must be Novopetrovsk!

DYADIN: *(Shouting.)* Semyon! Run up to the milldam and see if you can see what's burning. Maybe from there...

SEMYON: *(Off.)* It's the forest of Telibeyevsk that's burning!

DYADIN: *(Shouting.)* What?

SEMYON: *(Off.)* The forest of Telibeyevsk !

DYADIN: The forest...

(Long pause.)

KHRUSHCHOV: I should be there...I must go to the fire. Goodbye!...Forgive me, I've said too much – but I couldn't help it, I've never felt as low as I feel today...There's such a weight on my heart...but what difference does that make!...One must stand up and be a man. I'm not going to shoot myself, or throw myself under the mill wheel... No, I'm no hero, but I will become one! I'll spread my wings and be an eagle, and nothing will stop me, not this red glow, not the devil himself! If the forests burn down, I'll plant new ones! If she doesn't love me, I'll love another. *(He goes out quickly.)*

YELENA ANDREYEVNA: What a fine man he is!

ORLOVSKY: Yes..."If she doesn't love me, I'll love another!" I wonder what he could possibly mean by that?

SONYA: Take me away from here...I want to go home...

SEREBRYAKOV: Yes, it's time to go. It's so damp here, much too damp for me. Where did my lap-robe go?...And where's my coat?

ZHELTOUKHIN: Your lap-robe is in the carriage, and here is your coat. *(He helps him on with it.)*

SONYA: *(With great emotion.)* Take me away from here...take me away...

ZHELTOUKHIN: I'll take you.

SONYA: No, I'll go with Godfather. You take me, Godfather dear.

Act IV

ORLOVSKY: Let's go, little one, let's go. *(He helps her on with her coat.)*

ZHELTOUKHIN: *(Aside.)* Damnation! How disgraceful! How humiliating!

(Fyodor Ivanovich and Yulya begin putting the dishes and napkins in the basket.)

SEREBRYAKOV: There's a pain in the ball of my foot, my left one. It's rheumatism, no doubt about it...I'll be up all night again.

YELENA ANDREYEVNA: *(Buttoning his overcoat.)* Ilya Ilyich, my dear, will you fetch my cloak for me – and my hat? They're in the house.

DYADIN: But of course. *(He goes into the house and shortly returns with her hat and cloak.)*

ORLOVSKY: *(To Sonya.)* You're not frightened of the fire, my little one? Don't be afraid, it's not as red as it was. It must be dying down.

YULYA: There's half a pot of cherry jam left over...Oh, well, Ilya Ilyich won't let it go to waste. Take the basket, Lyonichka.

YELENA ANDREYEVNA: I'm ready. *(To her husband.)* Well, take me, O Statue of the *Commendatore*, and plunge with me into your twenty-six dismal rooms. Such is my lot!

SEREBRYAKOV: Statue of the *Commendatore*...I might find this comparison amusing, if it weren't for the pain in my foot. *(To all.)* Goodbye, my friends! Thank you for your gracious hospitality and for your pleasant company...A lovely day, a splendid picnic – everything is perfect, except – forgive me – there's just one thing I cannot go along with – and that's this provincial philosophy of yours, and your way of looking at things. What you need, ladies and gentlemen, is to do things. You cannot go on like this! You must do things...Yes...Farewell. *(He leaves with his wife.)*

FYODOR IVANOVICH: Let's go, little manager. Farewell, Pater. *(Fyodor Ivanovich and Yulya go out.)*

ZHELTOUKHIN: *(Following with the basket.)* Damn this basket! This is heavy!...I hate picnics. *(He goes out. Off.)* Alexei! Bring it around!

ORLOVSKY: Why are you sitting down, my little charmer? Let's go...*(He and Sonya begin to leave.)*

DYADIN: *(Aside.)* And nobody even said goodbye to me!...Remarkable! *(He blows out the candles.)*

ORLOVSKY: Now what is it?

SONYA: I can't go, Godfather dear...I don't have the strength! Oh, I'm so unhappy, Godfather...I'm just desolate! I can't bear it!

ORLOVSKY: *(Alarmed.)* What's wrong? My sweetheart, my beauty...

SONYA: Let's not go...Let's stay here a little longer.

ORLOVSKY: First, "take me away," then, "let's stay" – I don't know what you want...

SONYA: I lost my happiness here today...I can't...Oh, Godfather dear, I wish I were dead. *(She embraces him.)* Oh, if you only knew, if you only knew!

ORLOVSKY: You need a little drink of water. Let's sit down...Come...

DYADIN: Sofya Aleksandrovna, what's wrong? Oh, Mamachka!...I can't...I'm trembling... *(Tearfully.)* I can't take it...My baby...

SONYA: Ilya Ilyich, my dear one, take me to the fire! Please!

ORLOVSKY: To the fire? Why? What will you do there?

SONYA: Take me, I beg you, or I'll go myself. I'm desperate... Oh, Godfather dear, I can't...I can't bear it! Take me to the fire!

KHRUSHCHOV: *(Enters quickly, shouting.)* Ilya Ilyich!

Act IV

DYADIN: Here I am. What is it?

KHRUSHCHOV: I can't go on foot. Give me a horse.

SONYA: *(Happily.)* Mikhail Lvovich! *(She goes to him.)* Mikhail Lvovich! *(To Orlovsky.)* Go away, Godfather dear, I must talk to him. *(To Khrushchov.)* Mikhail Lvovich, you said you'll love another...*(To Orlovsky.)* Go away, Godfather dear. *(To Khrushchov.)* Well, I *am* another now...No more holding back...Only the truth, the simple truth. I'm in love, love you...I love you.

ORLOVSKY: *(Roaring with laughter.)* Well, well, here's one for the books!

DYADIN: Isn't this delightful?

SONYA: Go away, Godfather dear. Yes, yes, only the truth, the truth...Well, say something, say something...I've said everything...

KHRUSHCHOV: *(Embracing her.)* My angel!

SONYA: Don't go, Godfather dear...Oh, Misha, whenever you tried to talk to me about love, I could hardly catch my breath for happiness – but I held back, I couldn't break free, out of fear and prejudice. They kept me from opening my heart to you just as they are keeping my father from welcoming Yelena. But now I'm free...

ORLOVSKY: *(Roaring with laughter.)* At last! What harmony! Made it safe ashore! Allow me to congratulate you. *(He makes a low bow.)* Oh, you shameless things! Shameless! Such dawdling, dragging each other along by the coattails!

DYADIN: *(Embracing Khrushchov.)* Mishenka, my little dove, how happy you have made me! Mishenka –

ORLOVSKY: *(Hugging and kissing Sonya.)* O my sweetheart, my little canary, my own godchild...*(Sonya bursts out laughing.)* There she goes again!

KHRUSHCHOV: Wait a minute, my head is spinning...Let me talk to her a little...Leave us alone...Please, please, go away!

The Wood Demon

(Fyodor Ivanovich and Yulya are heard approaching.)

ORLOVSKY: Shhhh! Quiet, children! Here comes my bandit! Let's hide, everybody, quick! Quick! (*Orlovsky, Dyadin, Khrushchov and Sonya all hide.*)

FYODOR IVANOVICH: *(Entering with Yulya.)* I left my whip around here somewhere. And a glove.

YULYA: You lie about everything!

FYODOR IVANOVICH: All right, I'm lying...So what? I don't want to take you home just yet. We'll have a little walk, and then I'll take you.

YULYA: You're a constant worry to me, nothing but trouble. *(She claps her hands together in surprise.)* Isn't Waffles a silly fellow! Look, the table hasn't even been cleared yet! Someone could walk away with the samovar...Oh, Waffles. Waffles! In spite of his advanced age, he hasn't the sense of a child!

DYADIN: *(Aside.)* We thank you kindly.

YULYA: As we came in, I heard someone laughing.

FYODOR IVANOVICH: Probably peasants, bathing. *(He picks up a glove.)* Somebody's glove...Sonya's...She certainly made a spectacle of herself today. She's in love with Wood Demon, mad for him, and he, that blockhead, doesn't even notice.

YULYA: Now where are we going.

FYODOR IVANOVICH: To the dam...We'll have a walk. It's the prettiest spot in the whole district...What a view!

ORLOVSKY: *(Aside.)* My son, my beauty, my bearded wonder...

YULYA: Did you hear that? Somebody's here.

FYODOR IVANOVICH: It's a miraculous place. Wood demons wander about, mermaids sit in the branches...Yes, Uncle, that's how it is. *(He slaps her on the shoulder.)*

Act IV

YULYA: I'm no uncle.

FYODOR IVANOVICH: Let's discuss this calmly. Listen, Yulichka – I've gone through fire, water, and copper pipes...I'm already thirty-five years old, and I have no real occupation in life, except as a lieutenant in the Serbian Command. In the Russian Reserves, I'm only a corporal. I'm a feather for every wind that blows...I must change my life, and, you know...you see, I have this idea, and I can't get it out of my head, that if I got married, my whole life would be turned completely around...So how about it, what do you say? For me, there's no one better.

YULYA: (*Bashfully.*) Uh...Well, you see...You must change first, Fedyinka.

FYODOR IVANOVICH: Sure, but don't be a gypsy! Yes or no.

YULYA: But I can't just...(*Looking around.*) Wait! Someone might see us, someone might be listening...Isn't that Waffles at the window?

FYODOR IVANOVICH: No, there's nobody there.

YULYA: (*Falling into his arms.*) Fedyinka!

(*Sonya bursts out laughing. Orlovsky, Dyadin and Khrushchov roar with laughter, applaud, and shout, "Bravo! Bravo!"*)

FYODOR IVANOVICH: Whew! You scared us! Where did you come from?

SONYA: Congratulations, Yulichka, good for you! And me, too! Me, too! (*Laughter, kisses, and general jubilation.*)

DYADIN: This is delightful! Delightful!

CURTAIN

The End

❖ PRONUNCIATION GUIDE ❖

LEONID STEPANOVICH ZHELTOUKHIN
lyeh-oh-NEED styeh-PAHN-oh-veetch zhel-TOO-heen

Leonid Stepanich
lyeh-oh-NEED styeh-PAHN-eetch

Lyonya
LYOAN-yuh

Lyonichka
LYOAN-eetch-kuh

YULIYA STEPANOVNA
YOO-lee-uh styeh-PAHN-uhv-nuh

Yulya
YOOL-yuh

Yulichka
YOOL-leetch-kuh

Yulka
YOOL-kuh

VASSILI
vuh-SEE-lee

YEGOR PETROVICH VOYNITSKY
yeh-GOR peh-TROH-veetch voy-NEET-skee

Zhorzh
ZHORZH

Zhorzhinka
ZHOR-zheenk-uh

IVAN IVANOVICH ORLOVSKY
ee-VAHN ee-VAHN-uh-veetch or-LOFF-skee

ILYA ILYICH DYADIN
eel-YAH eel-YEETCH DYAH-dyin

SERGEY NIKODIMICH
syair-GAY neek-uh-DEE-meetch

FYODOR IVANOVICH ORLOVSKY
fee-OH-der ee-VAHN-uh-veetch or-LOFF-skee

Fyodor Ivanich
fee-OH-der ee-VAHN-eetch

Fedya
FEHD-yuh

Fedyinka
FEHD-yeenk-uh

Fedyusha
fehd-YOO-shuh

Fedyushka
fehd-YOOSH-kuh

SOFYA ALEKSANDROVNA
SOH-fyuh ahl-eck-SAHN-druhv-nuh

Sonya
SOAN-yuh

Sonichka
SOAN-eetch-kuh

Sophie
soh-FEE

ALEKSANDER VLADIMIROVICH SEREBRYAKOV
ahl-eck-SAHN-der vluh-DEE-mer-veetch syeh-ree-bree-KOFF

Sasha
SAH-shah

MARYA VASSILIYEVNA VOYNITSKAYA
MAHR-yuh vuh-SEEL-yehv-nuh voy-NEET-skah-yuh

YELENA ANDREYEVNA
yihl-YEHN-uh ahn-DREH-yehv-nuh

Lenochka
LYEHN-uhtch-kuh

Helène
eh-LEHN

MIKHAIL LVOVICH KHRUSHCHOV
mee-hah-EEL LVOH-veetch hroosh-CHOFF

Misha
MEE-shuh

Mishenka
MEE-shehn-kuh

SEMYON
seem-YOHN

Syenka
SYEHN-kuh

NAZARKA
nah-ZAHR-kuh

SERGEY MIKHAYLOVICH SOLOVYOV
syair-GAY mee-HIGH-luh-veetch suh-luhv-YOFF

KHARKOV
HAHR-koff

PAVEL ALEKSEYEVICH
PAH-vyehl ah-leck-SAY-uh-veetch

BATIOUSHKOV
BAH-tyoosh-koff

TURGENEV
toor-GAY-nyeff

LOUKA
loo-KAH

GERASIM
geh-RAH-seem

YEFIM
yeh-FEEM

ZHUCHKA
ZHOOTCH-kuh

TRESOR
treh-ZOHR

KASHKINAZY
kahsh-kee-NAH-zee

OBLOMOV
ah-BLOHM-off

KIRPICHOV'S
keer-pee-CHOFFS

KUSNETSOV
kooz-neht-SOFF

LOMONOSOV
luh-muh-NOH-soff

ARCHANGELSK
ahr-HAHN-gyehlsk

AIVAZOVSKY
eye-vuh-ZOFF-skee

SHIMANSKI
shee-MAHN-skee

GRIGORI ILYICH
gree-GOR-ree eel-YEETCH

KONSTANTIN GAVRILICH NOVOSYELOV
kohn-STAHN-TEEN gahv-REE-leetch noh-voh-SYEH-loff

DMITRI PAVLOVICH
DMEE-tree PAHV-luh-veetch

ALEKSEYEVSK
ah-leck-SAY-ehvsk

NOVOPETROVSK
noh-vuh-pee-TROFFSK

TELIBEYEVSK
tehl-ee-BAY-ehvsk

MAMACHKA
MAH-muhtch-kuh

ALEXEI
ah-leck-SAY

NOTE: *Occasionally, in conversation, the patronymics may lose a syllable, informally – Fyodor Ivanovich becoming Fyodor Ivanich, Leonid Stepanovich becoming Leonid Stepanich, etc.*

A MIRACULOUS PLACE

"...a secluded corner of the world, a place of enchantment."

That's how Ilya Ilyich Dyadin, familiarly known as Waffles, describes his "domain" when he invites the other characters to pay him a visit. He lives in a house in the forest, beside a water mill. "In the nighttime," he tells them, "one can hear the mermaids splashing."

Fyodor attempts to take advantage of both the seclusion and the enchantment of this magical place as he romances Yulya, and his ironical remarks seem to correspond with Waffles' characteristic flow of sweet hyperbole. "It's a miraculous place," Fyodor says, paraphrasing Pushkin. "Wood demons wander about, mermaids sit in the branches..."

We might discount the testimony of Waffles and Fyodor, for different reasons, but by this time we ourselves have undertaken an expedition to the mill and we know these romantic images are true. A Wood Demon has been wandering about—the young doctor Mikhail Khrushchov, called so on account of his crusading passion to preserve the forests. He is even then hiding behind a tree, spying on Fyodor. As for the mermaid, the professor's unhappy young wife Yelena has only just abandoned her temporary nest among these very branches.

We know, or feel, that something magical is occurring, or about to occur, here, at this charged point beside the mill, a picturesque but potentially dangerous place. Coterminous worlds mysteriously intermingle. Significant transformations—Peter Quince would call them "translations"—are at hand. Lives may be lost, or found, or changed—even perhaps our own, for we now find ourselves taking place in this taking place. It is the particular magic of the theater, alive, and there is nothing like it. We are moving through time (living, dying) with these characters whom we have come to know so well, and we do find ourselves translated (more alive, more aware of being alive) as they work out their destinies. This mysterious process is as "charming," in the deepest sense of that ambiguous word, as Waffles thinks it is. THE WOOD DEMON offers a profound reconciliation, a joyous renewal, and we are full participants, as if we too have drawn our breath and had our being beside this mill; as, in fact, we have.

In this reading, THE WOOD DEMON is a finished masterpiece worthy to stand beside THE SEAGULL, UNCLE VANYA, THE CHERRY ORCHARD, and THE THREE SISTERS. It differs from them primarily in that it is young, a young man's play, overflowing with laughter, romance, noble aspirations, high spirits, hope. The sky has not yet come down around the ears of Chekhov's characters, and the possibility of grace—changing oneself, changing society—still exists. If this is true, the appropriate comparison for THE WOOD DEMON is not UNCLE VANYA, even though they have characters, situations, and dialogue in common, but with Shakespeare's A MIDSUMMER NIGHT'S DREAM, Mozart's THE MARRIAGE OF FIGARO, Bergman's SMILES OF A SUMMER NIGHT. Like those great Comedies, THE WOOD DEMON is a richly textured work of vigorous affirmation; its resolution has the power to heal.

FATHERLY PRIDE

> ...I beg of you, dearest Aleksander Ivanovich, don't be angry with me: I cannot allow THE WOOD DEMON to be published. I despise this play and am trying to forget I ever wrote it. Whether it is the fault of the play itself or of the particular circumstances under which it was written and first performed, I do not know, but it would be a severe blow to me if anyone tried to revive it. Here is a perfect example of the complete perversion of fatherly pride.
>
> —from a letter to Prince Aleksander Ivanovich Urusov, 16 October 1899, Yalta (This and all subsequent passages from the letters quoted in this afterword have been newly translated by Saunders and Dwyer.)

If THE WOOD DEMON is a neglected masterpiece, it must be admitted that the chief reason for that neglect is Chekhov's own absolute and unyielding rejection. Whoever resurrects THE WOOD DEMON, in print or on stage, does so in clear defiance of the master's strict injunction; when he was alive to suppress it, he did so.

Nicholas Saunders and I have the deepest respect and affection for Anton Pavlovich Chekhov, but his renunciation of THE WOOD DEMON could not have the force of law with us because the play itself—so exuberant, so illuminating, so vividly alive—had already won our hearts. Writers sometimes undergo changes that cause them to reject early work, but those who love them may well love them at every stage. We can thrill to John Donne's magisterial sermons, for example, without having to give up the altogether different thrill of "To His Mistress, on Her Undressing," however much the early poem might have embarrassed the venerable dean. In the same spirit, and without in any sense rejecting the poetic mastery of the later plays, Nicholas and I have tried to be faithful to the bright young man who wrote THE WOOD DEMON, with real pleasure and excitement, and a keen sense of doing something significant and new, in 1889, his twenty-ninth year.

If we examine the "particular circumstances" under which THE WOOD DEMON was written and first performed, we can perhaps come to see how a father might disavow such a star-crossed child, of whom so much had been expected.

The first mention we have of the play that would come to be called THE WOOD DEMON is in a letter Chekhov sent on 18 October 1888 to his friend Alexei Sergeyevich Suvorin, a successful pulp-press publisher and sometime-playwright. The letter reveals that Chekhov was planning to write a play in collaboration with Suvorin, and it includes descriptions of the proposed characters. (There were eleven. Eight of them did appear in THE WOOD DEMON, and four of those moved on to UNCLE VANYA).

In 1888, Chekhov was helping to support his parents and several siblings by slaving away at two professions, medicine and literature. He was an indefatigable writer of stories, for which he had already achieved considerable reputation, and he had also written some very popular one-act farces (he said he made more in a year from his dead BEAR than a gypsy could with a live one). The previous year he had had a great theatrical success with his melodramatic, full-length IVANOV. His more discriminating friends told him he wrote too much and too fast (three or four pieces a week) to write as well or as profoundly as he could, and he agreed. Only now, however, was he beginning to have enough financial security to take more time with his work. He started writing a novel.

Suvorin soon dropped out of the proposed collaboration, but Chekhov kept him posted on his progress:
I'll write THE WOOD DEMON in May or August.

Pacing back and forth, eating my dinner, I've managed to rough out the first three acts all right, but I've barely begun to think about the fourth. The third act is so scandalous that you will look at it and say: "This was written by a very sly fellow without an ounce of pity"
—to Suvorin, 5 March 1889, Moscow

Two days later, however, he sent contradictory messages to other friends:
I'm not writing a play now or planning to write one soon, because I have no particular subject in mind and no wish to write one. In order to write for the theater, you must love everything about it; without that love, you can't achieve anything worthwhile...Starting next season, I'll go see a lot of plays and teach myself how to write them.
—to Vladimir Alexeyevich Tikhonov, 7 March 1889, Moscow

I will not write plays. If I have some free time, I will do something *pour manger.* This fall and winter I will stick to fiction. The mere glory of being a playwright is not enough for me.
—to Alexei Nikolayevich Pleshcheyev, 7 March 1889, Moscow

Nevertheless, he was soon sending Suvorin ambiguous and playful reports:
Out of sheer boredom and the inability to work on a novel, I've begun to write THE WOOD DEMON. So far, it's as boring as NATHAN THE WISE. Sooner or later, however, I assure you, I will hold up some theater manager to the tune of four or five thousand rubles in one season. Oh, from what a great height I'll look down on you then!
—to Suvorin, 17 April 1889, Moscow

Can you believe it, I have finished the first act of

THE WOOD DEMON. It's not too bad, I think, but
it's long...It will be finished by the first of June.
Look out, you managers! You'll soon owe me five
thousand rubles. The play is very strange, and I'm
surprised to find myself writing such a strange
thing...
     —to Suvorin, 4 May 1889, Sumy

...The play turns out to be pretty boring, a kind of
mosaic, but it still gives the impression of some
good, hard work. I think I've invented some
entirely new characters. There isn't a single waiter,
or standard comic type, or cheerful little widow in
the whole play. The cast consists of eight, and only
three of them are incidental. I've tried to avoid
anything superfluous, and I think I've succeeded.
In a word, what a good boy am I, am I not? If the
censors don't crack my skull, you can look forward
to more pleasure from this play next season than
you would get by standing at the very top of the
Eiffel Tower and looking down on Paris.
     —to Suvorin, 14 May 1889, Sumy

The process had its downs as well as ups, of course:
     I started to write a comedy, but gave it up after
     two acts. It turned out to be boring, and there's
     nothing more boring than a boring play. I seem
     only capable of writing boring plays, so I might as
     well not write them.
          —to Tikhonov, 31 May 1889, Sumy

The excitement Chekhov sometimes felt is apparent in this
letter to his friend Pleshcheyev, the elderly poet who was
fiction editor of the NORTHERN HERALD:
     Believe it or not, I'm writing a full length romantic
     comedy, and I've already rattled off two and a
     half acts...I'm introducing good, healthy people, and
     half of them are very agreeable. There is a happy
     ending, and the overall tone is sheer lyricism. It is

called THE WOOD DEMON.
—to Pleshcheyev, 30 September 1889, Moscow

He seems so pleased with himself that this letter, only two weeks later, can't help but startle:

> Right after I finished my last story, though I was completely exhausted, my momentum kept me going and I wrote a four-act WOOD DEMON. I wrote it new, after destroying everything I'd written in the spring. I wrote with great pleasure, even with delight, despite the fact that my elbow kept aching and the spots in front of my eyes were colossal. Svobodin arrived and took the play away for his benefit night...
> —to Suvorin, 13 October 1889, Moscow

Pavel Matveyevich Svobodin had appeared in the celebrated second production of IVANOV at St. Petersburg's Aleksandrinsky Theatre in January of 1889. When he asked Chekhov for a new play to use on his benefit night, Chekhov offered him THE WOOD DEMON. Chekhov also promised the play to the actor Aleksander Pavlovich Lensky, of the Moscow Maly Theatre, for his benefit.

STICK TO STORIES

Chekhov's high hopes were soon dashed. Both theaters rejected THE WOOD DEMON, and the nature of those rejections stung the young playwright severely. He had particularly high expectations of the Aleksandrinsky Theatre, where his great admirer, the elderly author Dmitry Vassilyevich Grigorovich sat on the Selection Committee. Eight days after Svobodin had taken the play to the Aleksandrinsky Committee, Chekhov had heard nothing official, and he shows his anger in a letter to Pleshcheyev:

> I haven't heard a word about my play. Whether the

mice have nibbled it up, or the management has donated it to the public library, or whether it has burnt up from shame at the lies of Grigorovich, who loves me like his own son, anything is possible, but I know absolutely nothing! I have received no notice and have been given no reason from anyone. I do not know a thing, and I do not dare ask for fear of seeming to beg or of trying to get myself crowned with the laurels of the Alexandrinsky Theater, as if that were my deepest wish...A Petersburg newspaper reports that my play has been called "a beautiful dramatized narrative." Very nice. That means one of two things. Either I am a bad playwright (a verdict I readily accept), or all those people who love me like their own son and beg me for heaven's sake to be myself in my plays, to avoid cliches and present profound ideas, all those people are hypocrites.

—to Pleshcheyev, 21 October 1889, Moscow

In a letter sent four days later, Svobodin reaffirms his own support for the play but gives the Aleksandrinsky Committee's reasons for rejecting it; not enough action, too many "tedious" passages. Lensky's letter, which arrived soon after, was worse. The Maly Theatre had also rejected THE WOOD DEMON, and Lensky furthermore urged Chekhov to stick to writing stories, since he clearly had too little respect for "dramatic form" to be able to write plays. Nemirovich-Danchenko, who would as Stanislavsky's partner in the Moscow Art Theatre soon learn considerably more about Chekhov's playwriting talent, also sent a letter. It was no doubt meant to console and encourage. He thought that THE WOOD DEMON did not so much show Chekhov's scorn for the stage as reveal his ignorance of it. He thought it would be easy for a writer as accomplished as Chekhov to master the technique of writing for the stage, though he clearly had not yet done so.

In a reply to Lensky's letter, Chekhov wrote that he did

not intend to revise THE WOOD DEMON, and did not, in fact, plan to write any more plays.

He had already sent the play, however, to Suvorin, who sent back a detailed critique. Chekhov professed his gratitude:

> Thank you for reading my play. I knew myself that the fourth act was worthless, but after all, I did submit the play with the understanding that I would write a new one. More than half of your comments are of such value that I will definitely put them to use. Abramova wants to buy my play, and the offer is substantial. I guess I'll sell it. If it is staged, I will make so many changes you won't even recognize it.
> —to Suvorin, 12 November 1889, Moscow

Maria Moritsovna Abramova had a private theater in Moscow for one season which she managed with the actor Nikolai Solovtsov. Chekhov had written his triumphant farce, THE BEAR, for Solovtsov, and had dedicated it to him. The theater, in precarious circumstances, needed a strong play for the holiday season. Chekhov agreed to the terms, and sometime between the letter he wrote Suvorin on November 12 and the opening of THE WOOD DEMON on December 27, he found time to revise the first and third acts and to write an almost entirely new fourth act.

The new act was brilliant, magical. It should have made all the difference. The old fourth act (a draft copy survives) was indeed worthless, as Chekhov had told Suvorin. It was a careless attempt to tie up loose ends and get things over with in a hurry. It does not transport or enchant; worse, it reveals an incomplete understanding, at that stage, of many of the characters. In that painfully inept draft, we learn that Fyodor kidnapped Yelena at the end of Act Three, and then, angry at her escape, he beat up the peasant woman at whose hut they had stopped for water. This surly and unrepentant thug, so unlike the colorful, amusing, and sympathetic rogue of the final version, then shows up at the mill, demands that Serebryakov divorce the absent Yelena, and offers to duel Zheltoukhin and Khrushchov. Khrushchov himself turns out to be more like a sparrow than an eagle; he has a little fit of hysterics, and he encourages Sonya and Yulya to run around and scream, too. He says he feels better after his outburst, however, as the terrible tension has been broken. The ur-Serebryakov is a breast-beating penitent who accepts all the blame for everything. Worst of all, a servant of Orlovsky's comes in at the last minute to announce that the old man has just died. You'd think that would put some sort of damper on the happy ending, if you can call the tentative understanding that Sonya and Khrushchov reach a happy ending. Even so, they fare better than Yulya, who gets no similar resolution; Fyodor, suddenly reformed and grief-stricken, follows the servant home without a word to her.

To read the surviving draft of that fourth act is to understand how the Aleksandrinsky Committee and the managers of the Maly came to reject the play, and how Lensky and Nemirovich-Danchenko came to write those letters. Chekhov does seem either to scorn fundamental principles or to be ignorant of elementary stagecraft. How could the bold, true people of the first three acts be so tiresomely out of character in the fourth? THE WOOD DEMON was certainly not a masterpiece when Svobodin and Lensky carried copies off to Petersburg and Moscow. Chekhov knew that, however. He wrote Pleshcheyev that he did not consider a play ready for publication until it had been revised during rehearsals (27 November 1989), and he clearly expected to revise THE WOOD DEMON before or during the benefit rehearsals. When he had a chance to do exactly that, for the Abramova Theater production, he did produce a masterpiece. Surely the production would vindicate his method and proclaim his indisputable genius for the stage.

The production was not a success. Anton's brother Mikhail left a vivid description of the evening. He reported that the actress playing Sonya was too old and stout for the role: the audience laughed when the actor playing Wood Demon couldn't get his arms all the way around her in a hug. Worse, the clumsy red lighting effect created to suggest the forest fire also got laughs. The reviews were almost unanimously negative. Chekhov was again assailed for not knowing how to write a play, and for attempting to dramatize everyday life, the humdrum, the mundane. Ivan Ivanovich Ivanov, an important critic, asserted that ordinary conversations are actually boring: why should we go to the theater, he wondered, to hear people ask ten times about the health of a stranger. THE WOOD DEMON was withdrawn after three performances, but the revised text was published in Moscow in 1890. It is that text that is here translated.

Though Nicholas Saunders and I believe strongly that translations should not be "adaptations," which are in general impertinent, we have nevertheless made one addition to the 1890 text. We have restored from the draft text Serebryakov's first act monologue that begins "Hold your tongue and eat your pie." When Chekhov was revising THE WOOD DEMON, the play had few fans, and there may have been no one to encourage him to keep this long speech in an already long play. Again with the deepest respect, we've trusted Chekhov's first intuition. Hearing Serebryakov's ponderous attempt to socialize with the "nobodies" at Zheltoukhin's party vividly illuminates his character, amuses us, and increases the poignance of his complaints to Yelena in the second act about how much he hates his retired life.

TO BE AN EAGLE

Though Chekhov flourished in a time of political awakening, he was not political himself. He was a keen observer, of course, but with Trigorin's motivation: the compulsion to turn quotidian material into stories. He was therefore more absorbed by the concrete than the abstract and more interested in the telling detail than in the comprehensive system. When high-brow literary magazines began publishing his stories, his new liberal acquaintances criticized him for continuing his friendship with the pulp-press editor Suvorin, a conservative. In a letter to Plescheyev he denounced all such "labeling" as prejudice, and he gave his Wood Demon a speech elaborating that response, when Sonya calls him a "liberal":

> Everyone insists on seeing you as a "liberal," a "fanatic," a "crackpot"—anything you like, except a man. "Oh, I hear he's a fanatic!"—so pleased with themselves. "Oh, he's a crackpot!"—as if they'd just discovered America. And when they don't understand me and don't know precisely how to classify me, then they act as if I'm somehow to blame: "He's a strange fellow. Very strange! "...Whatever I am, look me straight in the eye, clearly, openly, without preconceptions, and, before anything else, try to see the real man in me—and in every man—or else you will never have peace.

Nevertheless, Chekhov was painfully aware of his own shortcomings, as he made clear in another letter five days later.

> I do not as yet have my own political, religious, and philosophical point-of-view, I change it monthly, and therefore I must limit myself to how my characters make love, marry, give birth, die, or talk.
> —to Grigorovich, 9 October 1888, Moscow

It is most interesting that Khrushchov, the character in all Chekhov's works perhaps closest to a self-portrait, does seem to have a firm political outlook. Wood Demon is a liberal, a visionary ecologist, with an almost obsessive passion to preserve the Russian forests and a keen sense of his own duties and responsibilities. Sonya worries that he may be a "fanatic," as "He never stops thinking and talking about his forests, and planting trees." She also frets about his peasant shirt—an admittedly eccentric touch for a young landowner in any nest of gentlefolk. "To speak bluntly," Sonya charges him, "you prefer the life of the peasant."

Chekhov's audience would have known from that peasant shirt that Khrushchov has been influenced by Count Leo Tolstoy, the great writer and social reformer, who preached a kind of levelling Christianity based on ethics, hard work, and renunciation. Tolstoy meant to generate religious and social reform as he called for a return to the simplicity of peasant life. A few years later, Chekhov wrote Suvorin that he himself had been profoundly influenced by Tolstoy, even obsessed with his teachings for a period of six or seven years. We don't know what period Chekhov meant, and there is little first-hand evidence of this obsession in his many surviving letters. Playful exaggerations often make those letters more vivid and colorful, and he probably exaggerated his debt to Tolstoy. Wood Demon, on the other hand, doesn't articulate the philosophical basis for his actions, but his words and actions allow us to infer a Tolstoyan program. "I work from early morning till late at night, summer and winter," he tells Sonya. "I don't have any peace. I fight with those who don't understand me. I suffer, sometimes more than I can bear..." Tolstoy's emphasis on renunciation, first of any sex outside marriage, later of any sex at all, might help explain the tenderly awkward, deliberately unromantic nature of the young doctor's proposal:

> I won't say I love you more than anything else in the world. For me, love is not everything in life...It is my reward! Precious girl, my dearest, for a man who works, struggles, and suffers, there could be no greater reward.

Chekhov may well have envied Khrushchov his Tolstoyan

leanings and his altruistic burdens. Look again at how he has Yelena praise him to Sonya:

> Forests are not the point. What matters, my dear, is that he has talent. Do you know what that means? Courage, clarity, generosity of spirit...When he plants a little tree or digs up a load of peat, he's already making plans a thousand years ahead, dreaming about the happiness of mankind. Such men are rare and must be loved.

Chekhov certainly worked as hard as Khrushchov, and gave of himself unstintingly, though he was torn between medicine and literature, not medicine and forests. He was an increasingly popular writer, but in his own mind his efforts were small, local, limited only to sustaining himself and those around him. Khrushchov, it should be pointed out, has no family depending on his labors, but what was Chekhov doing for the happiness of mankind a thousand years ahead? He could not know how posterity would treasure his stories. When the young Petersburg writer Ivan Leontievich Shcheglov ("Leontiev") sent him a review of the work of a number of young writers that included a favorable mention, Chekhov rejected the praise: "In our talents," he wrote, "there is plenty of phosphorus, but no iron. We are beautiful birds, I suppose, good singers—but we are not eagles." (22 January 1888, Moscow)

Khrushchov echoes this metaphor of eagles at the climax of the play. Led to reexamine his own heart and behavior by the catastrophe of Zhorzh's suicide and the disappearance of Yelena, whom he had so cruelly wronged, Khrushchov at first despairs. He describes his own shortcomings, and those of Serebryakov, who is also thought of as an authority, a leader:

> I'm just like everybody else...shallow, stupid...But you're no eagle yourself, professor! And, nevertheless, the people in this district—all the women, anyway—see me as a hero—and you, well, you're famous all over Russia. But if a man like me can really be thought of as a hero, and a man

like you really regarded as famous, it just means that in such a void any nobody can be a king. There are no true heroes, no men of real ability, there is no one to lead us out of the dark woods, to rebuild what we destroy, there are no true eagles who deserve their glory...

When he learns that the forest of Telibeyevsk is burning, however, Wood Demon's spirit rallies, and he ringingly articulates the philosophy of action that helps to set this play apart from those that followed:

I should be there...I must go to the fire. Goodbye!...Forgive me, I've said too much—but I couldn't help it, I've never felt as low as I feel today...There's such a weight on my heart...but what difference does that make!...One must stand up and be a man. I'm not going to shoot myself, or throw myself under the mill wheel... No, I'm no hero, but I will become one! I'll spread my wings and be an eagle, and nothing will stop me, not this red glow, not the devil himself! If the forests burn down, I'll plant new ones! If she doesn't love me, I'll love another.

Chekhov was bitterly disappointed by the response to THE WOOD DEMON, and in the aftermath he seems to have undergone a real soul-searching. He resolved (briefly) to write no more plays, abandoned his novel, expressed his dissatisfaction with the ephemeral nature of his previous fiction. He wanted to do more serious, more significant, work; to gain glory, and to deserve it; to be an eagle. But how? What was he to do? Khrushchov tells us to be eagles, but he doesn't tell us how to do it.

SAKHALIN AND AFTER

How should we live our lives? That is the fundamental question raised by THE WOOD DEMON. At the beginning of the play, most of the characters have found their own answers, if only just to keep themselves entertained in that immense landscape, to keep from throwing themselves under the mill wheel.

Marya Vassilievna, as Zhorzh puts it, "keeps one eye on the grave, and with the other searches through her wise little booklets for the dawn of a new life." She's so involved in her pamphlets that she doesn't even notice her son's terrible despair. Waffles manages to thrive by pretending: he lives in his own imagination, like a child, and continuously reinvents the world as the adventures of Waffles. Orlovsky has been born again: his answer is to open his heart and ask forgiveness "in the name of Our Lord Jesus Christ." Before his conversion, however, he says he lived exactly like his "beautiful boy" Fyodor, whose best answer has heretofore been an answer common to rich young men: drinking, gambling, seducing women.

Sonya, in love with Khrushchov, and Zheltoukhin, in love with Sonya, think of marriage as the answer. It is the usual answer, after all, in comedies and in life. Yulya dreams of love a little, but she seems content to care for her brother and find her satisfaction as a "fine little manager" of his estate. Serebryakov has been an academic *perpetuum mobile* since he became a professor, and "I'm still at it!" he complains. He connives at a villa in Finland, which will put him close to the heady intellectual excitement of Petersburg (and, incidentally, outside the reach of the Russian censors).

Only Zhorzh and Yelena Andreyevna have no answers. Zhorzh has rejected his old answer to this question, can't find a new one, and can't live without one. If only he had loved Yelena ten years earlier, when their union would have been possible. Now, he has only despair, a terrible sense of life wasted, and darkness ahead. Yelena, on the other hand, wears herself out analyzing her life and the lives of the others ("This is not a happy home," she says, twice). She struggles to make sense of it all, to find a remedy:

> ...You're an educated man, Zhorzh, an intelligent man, and it seems to me that you of all people should understand that it's not the bad people, criminals and traitors, who are ruining the world— it's the hostility between good people, it's secret envy, it's all the little cares and worries which are never seen by those who consider our house a kind of intellectual haven. Help me to reconcile us all. I'm too weak to do it alone.

Zhorzh's suicide leaves Orlovsky, Waffles, and perhaps Marya Vassilievna more or less unshaken. Orlovsky has not lost his serenity in the fourth act. For a believer, death is not to be feared, and a man who was troubled is now at peace. For Waffles, all events lose the power to hurt him and gain the power to entertain or nourish him in the alchemical crucible of his imagination. Unshaken by the tragedy of Act Three, Orlovsky and Waffles are able to midwife the changes of the Act Four.

Marya Vassilievna does not reappear—it would be impossible to achieve those changes in the presence of the bereaved mother. Khrushchov reports, however, that she is as she was, "still busy with her pamphlets, looking for 'inconsistencies.'"

How should I live my life? Zhorzh can't answer, and his suicide precipitates a general existential crisis. Yelena Andreyevna has fled to the mill and is desperately trying to figure out what course she should take for the rest of her life.

Yulya's sustaining routine has been smashed: "Some sleep, others stroll about, and all I do is work like a dog, day after day...I wish I were dead."

Luckily for her, Fyodor has also been reexamining his life

as he thinks about "Old Zhorzh." Carousing isn't much of an answer, he's beginning to realize; there might be a better one right in front of him, in Yulya, the lesser of two evils.

> I'm already thirty-five years old, and I have no real occupation in life, except as a lieutenant in the Serbian Command. In the Russian Reserves, I'm only a corporal. I'm a feather for every wind that blows...I must change my life, and, you know...you see, I have this idea, and I can't get it out of my head, that if I got married, my whole life would be turned completely around...

Wood Demon has an occupation in life, perhaps, but he also has a toad in his heart. He's been sitting at home, unable to work, wracked with shame at his treatment of Yelena. He has contempt for himself and all the others, too:

> Yes, I'm just like everybody else, a little man—but you're no giant yourself, professor. Zhorzh was a little man, too—his best idea was to blow his brains out. We're all little men!

Sonya, drawing precisely the wrong conclusion from the event, is on the verge of renouncing her hope of happiness to expiate, vaguely, whatever part she played in the tragedy.

The fourth act soon works its magic. Yelena returns to her twenty six dismal rooms with ironic resignation, and Serebryakov admits that he is very happy to have her back. With her to fuss over him, he can get back to work. There was a kind of love between this husband and wife at the beginning, and they are both wiser now. At the very least, Yelena will no longer be in such desperate isolation, cut off from the others. All have new reason to love and respect her, and to atone for their former behavior. Sonya and Wood Demon, Fyodor and Yulya—the couples finally are free to sort themselves out in a manner Waffles will not be alone in finding "delightful!"

Left out of the reconciliation, however, was Anton Pavlovich Chekhov. Khrushchov finds his renewal in taking an action: he'll be an eagle as he flies to save the forest. Serebryakov insists that his serious work has made him justly famous, and he admonishes everyone else to take action: "What you need, ladies and gentlemen, is to do things. You cannot go on like this! You must do things...Yes...Farewell., Another letter shows us how deeply dissatisfied Chekhov was with the way he was living his life:

> On the whole, my life is pretty boring, and at times I'm even beginning to feel hatred, which has never happened to me before. Long, stupid conversations, guests, people looking for a favor, the one-two-or-three ruble gratuities, the expense of getting back and forth to patients who can pay me nothing—in fact, everything's in such a hopeless muddle I feel like running away.
> —to Suvorin, December 23, 1888, Moscow

Whatever his motivations, in April, 1890, four months after THE WOOD DEMON closed, Chekhov did run away. Taking Serebryakov's advice (and emulating Khrushchov?), he followed the lead of his heroes and did something— something that startled everyone who knew him. He turned his back on his life in Moscow and set off on a 3-month, 5,000-mile journey, most of it without the benefit of railroads, across the country and through Siberia to the prison island of Sakhalin, with the intention of making a study of the true conditions of Imperial Russia's prisoners.

He had a rich adventure in Sakhalin, and he wrote his study. That story is told elsewhere. He didn't find the fulfillment in Sakhalin that Khrushchov expected to find when he went to Telibeyevsk to fight the fire. The day he got back, Chekhov wrote these lines to Suvorin: "God's world is good. We alone are bad....One must work, work—and the hell with everything else." (December 9, 1890, Moscow). This is a cry from a different world than that of THE WOOD DEMON. It strikes the chord of the later plays. Sonya and Vanya will try to solace themselves with work, and hope for peace at the end of it. Chekhov tried to forget THE WOOD DEMON, to suppress it with a vehemence that suggests more motivation than mere disappointment at its lack of success. It is as if the youthfulness, the hope, the energy, the prodigal passion, of the early play somehow shamed him. It was a transition play in every sense, written just as the writer and his work began to undergo sea changes. After Sakhalin, Chekhov was no longer the young man who wrote it, and he would write nothing else like it. It is surely the more precious for standing alone.

Not all the early reviews for THE WOOD DEMON were negative, by the way. Chekhov's friend Prince Urusov loved the play, and he never changed his mind. In a letter written just after he saw the celebrated Moscow Art Theater Production of UNCLE VANYA, he told Chekhov, sadly but firmly, "You have spoiled your WOOD DEMON." He said that UNCLE VANYA lacked the very thing that made THE WOOD DEMON so striking: the Act Three suicide ("...the hero is killed, and life goes on."). Urusov particularly missed Fyodor, and the dramatic return of Yelena Andreyevna, and the whole night scene by the river. He said that UNCLE VANYA was good, too, the best of what was then being written, but THE WOOD DEMON was better. THE WOOD DEMON was more surprising, he insisted, more daring, altogether more interesting. He reported, moreover, that many others agreed with him.

So far, by and large, posterity has not. It is not necessary, of course, to choose between these plays. How lucky we are to have both! With a deep bow to Anton Pavlovich, and a metaphorical tip of our caps to Prince Urusov, Nicholas Saunders and I are as happy as Waffles to introduce you to—or reacquaint you with—this neglected masterpiece.

The Antaeus Company was founded in December, 1990, by Dakin Matthews and Lillian Garrett-Groag, under the aegis of Gordon Davidson, Artistic Director/Producer of the Mark Taper Forum, to explore the possibility of creating a permanent classical repertory ensemble in Los Angeles. The Taper gave the Antaeus Company a Classics Lab workshop of THE WOOD DEMON at its developmental space in the John Anson Ford Theater in the spring of 1992: a two-and-a half week rehearsal period culminating in three open public rehearsals. The translators and the Antaeus Company wish to express their deepest thanks to Gordon Davidson. The lab, directed by Frank Dwyer, with music by Theo Saunders, set and lighting by D Martyn Bookwalter, and costumes by Susan Watanabe, was staged in the round with the following cast:

Aleksander Vladimirovich Serebryakov:	DAKIN MATTHEWS
Yelena Andreveyna:	LORRAINE TOUSSAINT
Sofya Aleksandrovna (Sonya):	ROSE PORTILLO
Marya Vassiliyevna Voynitskaya:	PADDI EDWARDS
Yegor Petrovich Voynitsky (Zhorzh):	LAWRENCE PRESSMAN
Leonid Stepanovich Zheltoukhin	
(Lyonya):	RAPHAEL SBARGE
Yuliya Stepanovna (Yulya):	JANELLEN STEININGER
Ivan Ivanovich Orlovsky:	ANDREW ROBINSON/
	JOHN ACHORN
Fyodor Ivanovich Orlovsky:	ERIC ALLAN KRAMER/
	MARCELO TUBERT
Mikhail Lvovich Khrushchov	
(Wood Demon):	DAVID DUKES
Ilya Ilyich Dyadin (Waffles):	JOHN APICELLA
Vassili/Vassilissa:	MARCELO TUBERT/
	FRANCIA DI MASE
Sergey Nikodeemich/Semyon:	JOHN ACHORN/
	ANDREW ROBINSON

Coordinating Producer: Roy Conli
Production Manager: Chris Lore
Stage Manager: Jill Ragaway
Production Assistant: Kathy Cavaiola-Hill
Assistants: Kathryn Bikle, Yona Levit, Susie Walsh
Light Board Operator: Julie Starr Whitaker
Master Electrician: Steven Dirolf

Wardrobe Mistress: Jan Hill
Crew: Robin McKee, Martin Russell, Corky Dominguez

In addition, the translators would like to thank the actors
who helped them discover these characters in a reading of
the play at the CSC Repertory Theater (New York City)
in 1985: Robin Miramontes, Allison Brennan, Marion
Schnabel, George Taylor, Andrew Weems, Ava-Maria
Carnevale, P. L. Carling, Patrick Egan, and Robert
Zukerman.

The translators also wish to thank Mary Scoville, Penny
Fuller, Lillian Garrett-Groag, Oskar Eustis, Christopher
Breyer, and Renee Leask.

This translation will have its premiere at the Mark Taper
Forum, with the Antaeus Company under the direction of
Frank Dwyer, in the spring of 1993-94 season.